This Book Belongs to

_____

_____

Order this book online at www.trafford.com
or email orders@trafford.com

Most Trafford titles are also available at major online book retailers.

Print information available on the last page.

ISBN: 978-1-4269-0501-8 (sc)
ISBN: 978-1-4269-8375-7 (e)

Trafford rev. 05/30/2015

 www.trafford.com
North America & international
toll-free: 1 888 232 4444 (USA & Canada)
fax: 812 355 4082

THE GREEN IMP

and other incredible stories
by
MARK KUMARA

22 Stories
Of Mystery and Magic
To Read to Your Children.

Also by Mark Kumara

(for children)

THE ELF IN THE DUSTBIN(20 short stories)

THE MAGIC DIDGERIDOO (Pantomime)

EL DONDIO AND HIS AMAZING TIME MACHINE

(Pantomime)

*For Peggy and Rosie, and children everywhere -
especially for those who remain children at heart.*

Contents

1

THE GREEN IMP

There is a special wood in the heart of England, some miles north of a canal near Oxford, which is a genuine fairy wood.

What is a fairy wood you might well ask?

Fairy woods are where fairies are born and raised, and taught how to look after flowers, trees and woodlands.

You should know that every flower or clump of flowers has a fairy to look after it. This is a fact. Many children, before they become grownups and forget all about being a child, can see them.

1

Every flower has its own fairy to help it grow and become as beautiful as nature intended it to be.

The fairies themselves are raised by caring elves. When old enough, they are trained in all the procedures of flower growth - especially in the making of perfume and beautiful colours. In due course each fairy is given its own special flower, wherever it might be.

Woods that are fairy woods are always very private places. They are also very pretty, having plenty of flowers for the young fairies to play amongst and learn about their flowers.

The fairy wood in our story, just north of Oxford, was full of tall majestic beech trees, old oak trees and spreading chestnut trees, as well as silver birches and smaller bushy trees such as hazels and elders.

In spring, which is always an important time for young fairies, there were large clumps of bluebells under the beech trees, anemones under the chestnuts, pretty white snow drops under the oak trees, and vast carpets of yellow primroses as far as the eye could see.

One day, though, a line of red pegs appeared in the wood. They marched ominously through the flowers, going right through the middle of the wood.

Hammered into the ground at the entrance to the wood a sign had been put up.

ROADWORKS FOR THE NEW MOTORWAY. It said. KEEP OUT.

There was consternation in the fairy wood. "What is going to happen to us?" The fairies cried out when they saw the notice board. "Our wood is going to be ploughed under to become a motorway!"

One bright elf had an idea. "Let's call on the green imp," he said. "He is not very caring like we are, being a bit impish. But he has his uses. Maybe he can persuade them to move the motorway somewhere else."

So, off they went to see the green imp who lived in a

little dell with his wife who was also on the impish side but not nearly as impish as the green imp himself.

I must explain, you see, that an imp is an elf that is a bit of a rebel - a kind of non-conforming elf, if you catch my drift. That is why he is called an imp.

The green imp was very alarmed when told of the news. He didn't want to lose his home, either. He said to his wife. "I am going out for a while, dear. I may be sometime. Don't wait up for me."

The green imp went along to where he was told the red pegs were, and sure enough, there they were, marching in a straight line right through the fairy wood.

"Hmm!" He said to himself. "I know what I'll do. I'll just move the pegs a little to the left of the wood and the motorway will miss it completely.

This he did. He spent all night doing it. Next morning the projected motorway had taken a distinctly bendy twist to the left, going over a hill and through a smelly swamp.

Next day, when a bulldozer came to start building the road it went over the hill into the swamp. It sank like a stone, the driver just managing to jump out in time. The bulldozer left behind a few bubbles to mark its downward descent into the depths of the marsh. It was never seen again. Another bulldozer followed it. It was also swallowed up by the ooze of the marsh. The men building the road soon realised there was something wrong.

They complained to the motorway chief surveyor who couldn't understand what had happened. He was sure he had plotted the route correctly.

He called his team together and once again they set up their theodolites.

A theodolite is a prism like instrument perched on three legs which is used in surveying to plot angles and road alignments. They spent some time setting up their instruments, then went off for a tea break.

All the while, the green imp had been watching. The moment he saw the surveyor and his helpers go off for their tea break, he nipped nimbly along and altered the settings on the theodolites so that the motorway would by pass the wood.

He was, indeed, a smart little imp!

As you can see, imps have their uses!

Next day, to his satisfaction, he saw the red pegs had taken a right hand bend which went past the woodland over a hill. Out of sight, behind the hill, there was an abandoned quarry.

The green imp was very pleased with himself.

When the bulldozers came the following day, the first one, a gigantic yellow monster with a roar like a major clanking earthquake, drove straight over the hill and, before it could stop, it toppled over the edge of the quarry. Again, the driver just managed to escape in time. But, the clanking monster took a dive, plunging with a tremendous splash into the lake which lay at the bottom of the old quarry, never to be seen again.

It was followed by a second just as hideous monster which with an even greater splash and a roar of exploding steam sank on top of it. The men quickly realised something was wrong.

"Sabotage!" They cried. "We want the police! We have lost four bulldozers! And four of our men have had a terrible fright!"

What was happening? Who was moving the pegs? Who was mucking around with the theodolites?

I must explain that imps are practically invisible. The fact is, you can't see them when you look at them. What I mean is, if you are looking at them - even if you don't know you are looking at them - you can't see them. There is only one way you can see them and that is *behind* you. But, you can't look behind you unless you look in a mirror.

That's why I said *practically* invisible. Not many people carry a mirror around with them just to look behind them. You wouldn't think of that, would you? As I have said...it's not practical!

So, the green imp went about his impish work utterly invisible to all and sundry.

To the site manager and the workmen it was all a total mystery.

The site manager did, however, persuade the local police to put a police car at the entrance to the wood over night.

Next morning, the green imp was intrigued to see the police car was still there. He crept up behind the car, curious to see what the policeman was doing.

The policeman was eating a doughnut and pouring himself a steaming cup of coffee from a thermos.

At that very moment, the policeman happened to look in his rear view mirror and saw an alien green face looking at him.

"Arrrgh!" He cried, spilling his coffee. He threw the remains of his doughnut out of the window, driving off with such a revving and spinning of wheels in the soft mud that it splattered all over the green imp. The terrified policeman vainly attempted to control his car which was now fish-tailing all over the slippery road. It side-swiped a road grader with a crash of scraping metal, spun off the road altogether and finished up nose deep in a heap of gravel where it came to a rather sudden and permanent halt.

"I saw a little green man. Horrible he was!" The policeman said to his Inspector when his Inspector appeared on the scene, looking at the crumpled car with a sour expression on his face.

"Hmm!" Said the Inspector. "Little green men, eh?"

"Horrible! Gave me a turn, I can tell you!"

"From Mars, was he?"

"Well, yes, come to think about it he did look like an alien! Sort of green!" The policeman shuddered. "I don't want to go back there, I don't!"

"Go on holiday for a long time," replied the Inspector. "Take a good long rest!"

By now, news of the terrible happenings at the site of the new motorway, began to actually make news in the local paper. Soon everyone was hearing about what was happening up at Fairy Wood, as it was called locally. Many people began asking why such a pretty wood had been chosen to have a motorway through it in the first place?

A petition was started and many people signed it. It soon became national news and even more people signed the petition.

SAVE FAIRY WOOD became a bumper sticker on many cars and children sent letters to politicians. But none of it did any good.

The Minister of Road Works came from London to see what all the fuss was about. He took a quick look at the wood and announced there was no good reason the motorway shouldn't go through the wood. "It is not as if the wood is being used for anything," he said. "It's just a wood. I have made a decision to continue with the road as planned. Any anyone who attempts to interfere with the building of the motorway, including those who have already tried, will be prosecuted to the full extent of the law."

As far as the Minister was concerned that was that!

But as far as the green imp was concerned *that* was far from *that*!

When his wife had cleaned the mud from the policeman's car off him and he had tossed back a small tot of elderflower brandy, and when he was looking a healthier shade of green, he said to her once again: "My dear, I have to go out again. This time it might be for an even longer time. Don't wait up for me."

He had a plan.

He planned to go to London with the Minister to see what could be done.

And, this is exactly what the green imp did. He crept into the Minister's big ministerial car just as it was leaving and they all drove off together, the Minister, his chauffeur and the green imp - the green imp being entirely invisible, of course, being in the front seat beside the chauffeur while the Minister read parliamentary papers in the back, in the luxuriously soft leather seats of his splendid car, all the way back to his home in London.

The Minister noticed nothing unusual…except there was a strange fragrance of flowers in the car. He rather liked it.

A very comfortable home the Minister had, too. The green imp wasn't sure what to do to make the Minister change his mind, but he thought something might occur to him overnight. He found a spare room in the house and had good night's sleep under a doona with pretty flowers all over it.

He woke up bright and early and went to the bathroom. In the bathroom he looked at himself in the mirror and had an idea. He would write the Minister a message. One he couldn't miss.

On the basin there happened to be a spray-can of shaving cream. Just the thing! He would try his hand at a bit of graffiti.

Feeling mischievous and triumphant - and, of course, impish - he sprayed on the mirror the words: SAVE FAIRY WOOD.

He thought for a moment, then underneath he

sprayed: OR THE GREEN MONSTER WILL GET YOU!

It looked magnificent. All he now had to was wait until the Minister went to the bathroom. Which, sure enough, he soon did.

After the Minister had finished peeing, he went to the basin as he usually did to have a shave, he looked up at the mirror, and froze.

Shaving soap was all over the mirror.

What a mess! Graffiti!

He looked closer. What was written there? *Green monster*, indeed!

Who had done this? Was it his house cleaner? She would be fired!

Was it one of his children? What a pathetic joke! No pocket money for them this week!

Everyone knew how sensitive he was about the matter of this wretched motorway which was causing so much trouble? It was ridiculous to consider changing its route at this late stage.

He got hold of a towel and began to clean off the distasteful mess.

The green imp, anxious to see whether his message to the Minister was having the desired effect, crept up behind him.

"Green monster, indeed!" The Minister was muttering to himself, as he wiped the soap off the mirror. " Green monster...ha ha ha! I'll give them green monsters! They'll be seeing green monsters all right, before I've finished with them!"

Wiping the last of the soap off the mirror, he suddenly saw a strange green face peering at him, over his shoulder right behind him.

He froze in absolute shock.

Then he gave a great cry: "Arrrgh...!"

He fled the bathroom as if all the hounds of hell were

after him, slamming the door so hard it made the whole house shake.

Racing down the corridor, he ran back to his bedroom.

Shivering with fright, he climbed back into bed with his wife.

"What on earth is wrong?" she asked. "You look as if you've seen a ghost."

"I have!" He gasped. "I have. It was green. A horrible green alien thing. A green monster!"

"What! In the bathroom?"

"Yes, yes! In the bathroom."

His wife was a very practical woman. She was a country girl at heart. She liked chasing after hares with beagles, in tweeds and gum boots. But this was some-thing new to her. She had never seen her husband in such a state. She supposed it was the all stress he had been under lately - about that wood in Oxford - what was it called? Yes, Fairy Wood!

"Dear, it might be better if you stayed in today. Not go to the House of Commons. Have you anything you could do at home?"

"Yes," he said, still shaking, but now thinking even harder. "In fact, I have. You know that Fairy Wood busi-ness? I have..." He shuddered. "I have...decided not to put it through the wood, after all."

"Good idea," she said. It will show you have a compassionate side to you. Not a bad idea in an election year. Also...," His wife continued, "It's not a bad idea to be seen as a little bit *green* these days."

He shuddered again. "Please don't mention the word *green!*" He closed his eyes, attempting to get rid of the image in the mirror. "I think I will stay at home today. I'll get to work on it straight away!"

So, that is how Fairy Wood was saved from being turned into a motorway.

On his return to the fairy wood the green imp found he was a hero.

However, the elves decided they couldn't turn him back into being an elf. He was far too impish for that!

Anyway, he liked being an imp and his wife liked him being an imp, too.

Which was definitely a good thing.

2

TOMMY'S SURFBOARD

For Tommy's birthday his parents gave him a boogie board. It was green on top and blue underneath.

But it had no strap. So, his father cut him a length of flex from a rusty old electric fire which didn't work anymore. It worked well as a strap.

One end of the strap was tied to the ring at the front of the board, the other end he made into a loop for Tommy to hold on to, so that if a big wave bowled him over, he wouldn't lose it in the surf.

Sometimes surfboards seem to have a mind of their own, don't you know - as I am sure you do if you have ever been surfing.

It is important to keep them under control.

However, and this is the thing, the truly amazing

thing as you will soon find out: Tommy's surfboard really *did* have a mind of its own.

As the summer passed, Tommy soon became good at surfing. He and his green boogie board (blue underneath) seemed to be going well together. Over the water they flew. Racing at great speed toward the sandy shore.

The water bubbled and sizzled furiously around Tommy's ears. What a fine sound it made. What a feeling it was. What could be more exhilarating! This was the life!

They were on to a good thing, for sure. Everyone thought so!

Except, that is, for the boogie board.

"Why?" The boogie board thought to itself, "Do I always have to be underneath. "Why can't I be on top for once? Why can't I be in control ?"

The boogie board became more and more disgruntled. It became morose. It took on a sluggish demeanour.

Tommy wondered if it had become water-logged.

But, no, it was just plain disgruntled, sluggish and morose. I am sure you have got the picture.

To put it bluntly, Tommy's boogie board was no longer happy being a boogie board; especially not Tommy's boogie board. It wanted to be something else. It wanted *out* of the partnership.

"Who wants to have someone lying on top of you all day long?" It said to itself. "It's *so* boring!"

It was becoming thoroughly depressed.

Then it had an idea.

"Hey! What if I was a proper surfboard - like one of those big boards that go whizzing past us looking so superior. What if I was like them? Wouldn't that be grand? I would be sure to be happy if I had a long pointy nose and a tail fin. Instead of *lying* on me, Tommy would be able to stand up. We could catch bigger and better waves farther out to sea, and go swooping past all the other boogie boards at terrific speed."

"What a marvellous idea!" Thought the boogie board.

Even as it thought about it, it began to change its shape. It grew a long pointy nose and a shiny metal tail fin. It grew longer and longer.

But, as it did so, the boogie board began to lose its beautiful blue and green colours.

It started to turn a dirty white.

Next morning, Tommy, as you can imagine, was surprised to find that his surfboard had disappeared.

In its place, in the garden shed, leaning up against the wheelbarrow was a strange, very tall, grey surfboard.

It had a pointy nose and a big metal tail fin, and looked as if it meant business - the business of serious stand-up surfing.

Tommy was amazed. Where had his lovely green and blue boogie board gone? Who could have taken it? Who had swapped it for this strange surfboard he was now looking at?

Tommy told his father that his boogie board seemed to have changed in the middle of the night into a stand-up surfboard, but his father thought Tommy was having a joke and wasn't interested.

Sitting at the kitchen table, enjoying his Sunday morning breakfast of coffee and croissants, his father was occupied in deciding whether to try the ginger or the grapefruit marmalade. He had just unrolled the morning paper. He wasn't to be disturbed.

Oh well, thought Tommy, maybe it's time I had a go at standing up on a surfboard, anyway.

Off he went to the beach and paddled out to the big waves as he had seen the expert surfers do.

After a few tumbles, he got the hang of it. In no time at

all, Tommy was standing on his grey surfboard, flashing down the front of big rollers, twisting and turning with the best of them.

What fun this was!

Now he was king of the waves! Swooping through the blue tubes, dazzling white foam curling above his head, and the surf sizzling all about him - this was the life!

He didn't mind losing his boogie board, one little bit. This kind of surfing was much more fun.

He didn't want to go back to lying-down surfing. No way!

He never dreamed, of course, that his new dirty white surfboard was really his old green and blue boogie board.

Tommy was soon an expert at stand-up surfing. Everyone thought so. Even his sister said he was wonderful.

The surfboard was not a happy surfboard, though.

"Why?" It said to itself, "Do people tell Tommy *he* is so wonderful. What about *me*? Why don't they tell me *I* am wonderful? Tommy wouldn't be able to go surfing at all without *me*. Are we not a partnership?"

He became disgruntled and morose again. It was unfair, he thought, that people didn't see what a wonderful surfboard he was. Also, he was getting fed up at being controlled by Tommy all the time. They always went where Tommy wanted to go. Always! Never where *he* wanted to go.

It seemed nothing had changed. He didn't feel happy at all.

"How would you like someone standing on top of you all day long, telling you when to go and when to stop?" He grumbled to himself.

"We never do what I want to do!"

The surf board became very sullen.

"How strange!" Thought Tommy. "It feels like it's getting sluggish like my old boogie board."

Tommy thought it must be water-logged. He stood it against the sunny side of the veranda to dry out in the wind.

"I'll leave it there for a while," he said.

And, there it remained for the rest of the summer. Tommy was learning to play tennis and he forgot about surfing. Tennis was great fun.

Weeks went by.

The surf board didn't like this one little bit. Seagulls came and sat on it and did messes. A lot of messes!

It got very angry.

It felt useless and left out. Left out, in fact, to become cracked in the sun, becoming dirtier by the day, and every day hating it more and more. Especially, it hated the screeching seagulls and their smelly messes.

Ugh! Ugh! Ugh! Triple Ugh!

The surfboard was working itself into a rage.

Then, one day, there was no tennis. From the window of his bedroom Tommy saw big blue rollers with translucent green centres and dazzling-white tops, moving majestically toward the shore.

A perfect surfing day!

He grabbed his surfboard and ran all the way to the beach.

The surfboard was still in a bad mood.

"But at least," it thought to itself, "Anything is better than being left out in the sun. I won't have seagulls doing their messes on me!"

Tommy paddled out and soon found some magnificent waves to ride on.

There was even a pod of dolphins surfing next to him.

"This is the life!" He shouted out to the sky as he

swooped and soared on the moving sea. "I am king of the world!"

The dolphins were having a great game surfing beside him, flipping themselves over the same waves he was riding just before the waves crashed to the shore.

Tommy loved watching them. They looked so happy and frolicsome. And powerful. Awesome!

"And *free*," grumbled the surfboard. "They are free! Unlike *me*!"

The surfboard decided that at the first opportunity it would become a dolphin.

Then, at that very moment, Tommy, who was watching the dolphins, lost his concentration. He fell into a deep trough. A wave crashed over him. He tumbled over and over in the skirling foam.

Whiteout!

When, at last, Tommy got his head above water and got his breath back, he realised straight away that his surfboard had gone. It had broken free.

He was still holding on to the old piece of flex his father had tied to the board, but the surfboard was no longer attached to it.

It was nowhere to be seen.

Tommy made for the shore. He looked for it along the beach. But, no, it hadn't been washed up on the beach. Then, he went back into the deeper water and searched for it there, but no one had seen his surfboard anywhere.

Now, as you probably realize, the surfboard didn't want to be found. It wanted to be free.

"I want to be a dolphin," it said.

As it held this thought in its mind, the surfboard began to change.

Unfortunately, it still had a lot of angry thoughts in its mind. So, instead of changing into a happy dolphin, it changed into an angry shark.

It grew a big grey fin on its top side and many nasty-looking teeth.

"Ha!" It said to itself. "Now I am free. Now I am powerful. Now I am someone to be reckoned with.

Oh dear me, this was an unhappy state of affairs.

Because, suddenly, there was a shark in the water.

Everyone started screaming and yelling, and pointing and waving, at the shark that had suddenly appeared out of nowhere.

On the beach, lifeguards began jumping up and down, waving flags and blowing whistles. A siren blared its alarm over the bay.

Everyone was racing for the shore to get out of the water any way they could.

What a pandemonium!

But, what of the surfboard?

Well, let me tell you, it was having a wonderful time. With great glee it swam around frightening the wits out of everyone with its big grey fin, sticking out of the water, and its make-believe teeth.

At first, even the dolphins moved away from this strange creature which looked like a shark but wasn't a shark.

The surfboard was having the time of its life. It swam round and round at great speed chasing everyone out of the water.

"Don't be afraid," it cried out. "It's only a game. It's only a game! Please don't be frightened!"

But no one heard it. No one listened. Everyone was far too frightened.

Everyone, that is, except the dolphins who were not fooled quite as easily as all that!

Suddenly, there was no one left in the water. Only the surfboard remained, listlessly swimming about feeling, once again, lonely and useless.

"Maybe," it thought to itself, "I will drift around like

this for ever, drifting about until I fall to pieces. Maybe, I'll get waterlogged and sink. Or, more likely, I'll be smashed into pieces against some rocks."

It felt lonely and afraid, and began to cry.

After all, it had tried so hard to be free. It had tried so very hard. Did no one understand?

No one noticed because everyone was standing on the beach. There was already plenty of salty water in the sea. Who would notice a few extra tears?

But, the dolphins *had* noticed. They noticed everything going on in the sea.

And something else the dolphins had noticed which, in the general rush for the shore, no one else had seen, was a small girl with floaties on her arms, floating far out to sea.

A strong rip had her in its grip. It was taking her farther and farther out to sea.

All that could be seen of her was her tiny fair head and the occasional flash of her yellow floaties as she topped a wave.

The dolphins swam round and round the small girl in a circle, sending her loving thoughts.

But they didn't know what to do. She was so tiny.

"Fetch that silly surfboard that is pretending to be a shark," One of them suggested.

So that is what they did.

The biggest dolphin swam at great speed toward the surfboard, giving it quite a fright.

"Oh, no! This is the end." Said the surfboard to itself, "I am going to be smashed into pieces by this big brute. "I suppose it is what I deserve."

"Come on," said the dolphin. "Stop feeling sorry for your self. You have a job to do."

The dolphin took the broken piece of chord that was trailing behind the surfboard in its mouth. It pulled the surfboard along at great speed, giving the surfboard no time to object.

The big dolphin swam toward the small girl whose name was Trina.

Then, very gently, it nudged the little girl toward the surfboard until she was able to clamber on to it.

Trina's small hands clung tightly to the old piece of electrical flex. She was cold and tired, and shivering.

Then, the dolphins started jumping. They leaped out of the water again and again, both in celebration and to attract the attention of the lifeguards on the shore.

"Look at the dolphins jumping," some one cried out.

Everyone looked. No one had ever seen them leap so high before.

One of the lifeguards looked through his binoculars.

"Crikey!" He yelled out. "There's a little girl out there on a surfboard. "Come on everybody! Get the rubber ducky in the water. Quick sticks!"

Out roared the lifeguards in their rubber boat, the boat jumping through the white breakers like a big, bouncing, orange ball, its engine snarling.

It raced toward the little girl who was clinging to the surfboard as if her life depended on it. Which of course it did.

Now, a strange thing began to happen: the grey surfboard that had tried so hard to be free like a dolphin but had ended up as a peculiar kind of shark, began to change back into a boogie board.

It began to regain its previous bright colours.

The rubber boat, travelling at top speed, soon reached the small girl lying on the boogie board. The lifeguards saw that she was fine. Shivering a bit, but fine.

The dolphins swam around happily as both Trina and boogie board were rescued by the rubber ducky.

When the boat reached the shore, everyone came around

Trina was united with her mother who had just left the beach for a moment to take her brother to the toilet. She'd had no idea that Trina was floating out to sea, or that a menacing shark had been seen in the water scaring everyone to bits.

One of the lifeguards held up the boogie board. It was a sparkling iridescent green on top. Blue underneath. It had a short piece of electrical flex tied to it.

"Anyone know who's this is?"

"That's my boogie board," said Tommy. "I lost it. I haven't seen it for ages."

"It looks brand new." Said the life-guard. "It's a beauty! Done a good job, too. In future, you'd better hang on to it."

Unnoticed by anyone, a warm glow began spreading through the boogie board.

It suddenly felt amazingly happy.

3

FACE PAINTING

Michael's family were apple farmers. Their farm was next to a huge forest that stretched for hundreds of kilometres up the western side of Tasmania. It was - and still is - one of the oldest forests in the world.

Now, Michael's father was a hairy man. Incredibly hairy, in fact. He had thick black hairs on his chest, which Michael liked to tangle his fingers in, and a huge bushy black beard which was softer than it looked. His arms and legs were so hairy that after a swim he needed two towels to dry himself. Many people thought they had never seen such a hairy man.

His mother was a school teacher who taught at the local school.

There is a lot of wild land in Tasmania. The mountains have snow on them in the winter. Even in summer, the impenetrable rain forests on the western side of the island are wet and cold. Grey-white lichen hangs like stringy cobwebs from the ancient trees. Emerald green moss covers everything.

The forests are thick and dark. Animals like the fierce Tasmanian devil live in the gloomy undergrowth.

A few people say they have glimpsed a creature which looks like a striped greyhound with a pouch like a kangaroo. Was it a Tasmanian tiger?

Who knows?

But, one thing everyone is agreed on: the Tasmanian forests are the last forests in the world which remain in their original primal state. Anything could be living in them.

Michael's father, who was fond of telling stories, said he thought the Tasmanian tiger might still be lurking in the ancient forests. What other ancient animals might there be in their impenetrable depths, he wondered? Dinosaurs, perhaps. Ancient creatures hidden away and never before seen by anyone.

He made up marvellous tales of make-believe monsters, stories which were sometimes scary - but not too scary - which had Michael shivering in pretend-fear, laughing and giggling, pulling at his father's beard and wanting more of the same, before being tucked into bed at night.

Michael was a great giggler. He liked to make up his own stories and laugh at them. He could see the funny side of anything - especially if it was something that grown-ups took too seriously.

He had a best friend called Satya whose father was a doctor. Satya had been born in India and his family lived in the town where Michael went to school.

Michael and Satya did everything together. Anyone could see that Sat and Mike - as they were called by their friends - were great buddies.

They were planning to go camping together.

This was so exciting!

Everything was going well with their preparations for camping when, the very night before they were due to leave, a huge tree fell on the doctor's house in a storm.

Satya was killed by the falling marri tree.

When Michael was told about this, he nodded.

It was the very faintest of nods. His face froze up. He stared into space for a long while. Then he went into his room and closed the door.

Michael never talked - or smiled, or laughed again.

How sad this was.

His parents tried everything to make him talk or smile again. But nothing worked.

Michael still went to school, but he sat silently and listlessly at the front of the class. He didn't talk to anyone. He wrote his lessons in his book. He did his homework. But, more often than not, he just stared out of the window.

Occasionally, his one-time friends flicked paper balls or rubber bands at him. But, Michael just sat there passively. Expressionless, he didn't respond. They soon got tired of that.

It was as if a part of him had died along with Satya.

Would he ever talk again, everyone wondered?

His parents took him to see plenty of doctors. They took him to see a psychiatrist who gave him a lot of pills to take. The pills made him drowsy and feel like a zombie. They didn't work.

They took him to see a woman psychologist in Hobart who played games with him on the floor. She made him paint pictures - and told him stories to try and make him laugh or cry. That didn't work, either.

None of it was any use.

But he did learn to paint. He become good at painting.

But, still, he wouldn't talk or smile.

His father spent hours and hours reading him his favourite stories. He made up new stories, funny stories, and scary stories about other monsters in the forests.

But, nothing made Michael smile or talk, or giggle, the way he used to.

Everyone was sad that Michael had become the way he was.

A year went by.

People began to get used to the way he was.

Sometimes he wandered around like a ghost, but mainly he sat for hours on end just staring into space.

No one paid him any attention anymore.

Even his parents began to get used to this strange silent Michael. They were very sad about it. But, what could they do?

It was almost like he had become part of the furniture. Always there. But not really there, if you see what I mean.

He lived in a world of his own that no one was able to penetrate.

Well, as it happens, one day Michael's father announced that some big man from the Australian Government in Canberra was to visit them to look at their apple trees.

As it turned out, he was a small chubby man and wore big round glasses which made him look a bit owlish.

"A proper twit, if I've ever seen one!" His father remarked.

However, he was going to be staying for a few days, so they had to make the best of it.

Now, when the professor whose name was Gungabum saw they lived close to the ancient forest he was excited.

"I have heard rumours about a wild man in the forest," he said in a high jerky voice (the same way he moved abruptly around the room): "Maybe it is the missing link. The ape-man?"

It was on the tip of his father's tongue to say: "What utter rubbish!" But he thought better of it. It paid to keep in the good books of these bureaucrats.

He reminded himself: *We can put up with this windbag for a night or two. Perhaps I'll tell him a story about what really goes on in Tasmania!*

He chuckled wickedly.

Michael's mother got the spare room ready. And made a special pot roast for their guest.

As usual, Michael stood by, silently watching.

"What do you think is out there?" asked Professor Gungabum, " pointing vaguely toward the dark forest, whilst shovelling a spoonful of pot roast into his mouth.

"Ah!" Said Michael's father, stroking his nose. "Who knows what is in those forests."

"Yes! Yes!" Cried Gungabum excitedly, wiping the steam from the hot stew off his round spectacles. "Who knows what's in there. All that primal forest. Untouched. Unmapped. Anything could be in there. Right!"

"Only rumours...," said Michael's father.

"About what?"

"Big Foot. The yeti of Tasmania, some call it."

"The wild man of Tasmania," gasped Gungabum.

Michael's father nodded. "Just rumours," He said. "Just rumours. Myself, I don't believe a word of it."

The chubby little man nearly leaped off his chair in excitement.

"You don't say!"

"However," said Michael's father. "Something rather strange has been happening in my apple orchard recently. My apples have been disappearing and a few nights ago I caught a glimpse of a big hairy shape. What it was I cannot say."

"The ape-man!" Gungabum breathed.

Michael's father shrugged. "Who knows. But it was certainly big and hairy. Rather on the pale side, If I do say so myself. With gleaming red eyes."

"You saw its eyes?"

"Oh yes. Two big gleaming red eyes in a large pale face. With lots of black hair. Maybe some ginger."

"Oh my! Oh my! I must see this," cried Gungabum. "I will sit up tonight. All night if necessary. You must show me exactly where you saw it. I will need to find the best place to hide in your orchard."

Michael's father waved his hands. "If you insist," he sighed. "But I must warn you, this creature is very shy. You might have to sit out there for a long time, and it can get very cold out there at night."

But, Gungabum wouldn't listen. In his mind, he already had visions of a Nobel prize. He saw himself touring the world giving lectures on the Tasmanian yeti. The ape-man of Tasmania! Discovered by Professor Gungabum!

What an incredible sensation it would be...*he* would be!

He got ready his camera, put on his sheepskin coat and found a place to sit against an old apple tree in the orchard.

"Don't breathe heavily," warned Michael's father. Whatever it is, it is very sensitive. If you see anything, keep very quiet. Who knows what it might do. I have heard it is immensely powerful"

"Don't worry about me," Said Gungabum as he settled down with his binoculars and camera. "I have done this sort of thing before, you know."

"Oh, that's all right, then," said Michael's father

"What an ignorant man", Gungabum muttered to himself as he settled down. "No imagination!"

He sniffed, and sat against the tree.

Michael and his father returned to the house, with Michael, as usual, following quietly behind.

Back in the house, Michael's father whispered to his son. "Fetch me your paints. I have a plan."

When Michael had fetched his paints, his father said to him: "We are going to play a joke on this pompous ass."

He pulled down his trousers and bared his naked bottom. "I want you," he said to Michael, "to paint a face on my bottom with your paints. Some curly black hair all round and at the top, and a big red eye on each cheek will do. Nothing too fancy, mind. Make it as real as you like. Maybe put in some ginger hair."

Michael, without a word and with his usual deadpan expression, set to and created a magnificent hairy face on his father's bottom. Each eye on each side of his father's bottom was a wondrous fiery red, and the black hair curling around the gleaming cheeks had tints of ginger in it. He stepped back and looked at it.

His father was a hairy man, to be sure, but his bottom happened to be quite smooth. The paint had taken to it magnificently.

It was surely a fine piece of face painting. Or, should I say, bottom painting.

His father twisted himself around and peered at himself in the mirror.

He chuckled. "That's a masterpiece, Michael. Come on! Off we go into the orchard."

On tip toe, they reached the orchard by the long way round, entering the other side, just opposite where the professor from the mainland was sitting.

"This is where it gets a bit chilly," said his father in a whisper, beginning to remove his clothes.

Then, Michael's father got down on his hands and knees and began crawling backwards through the low bushes to where he knew Gungabum would be watching. He started to make peculiar grunting noises.

Gungabum was beginning to shiver in the frosty night.

It was hard leaning against the old apple tree which had knobbly bits on its trunk, and the ground was damp. He wished he had brought a cushion.

Suddenly he heard something moving in front him, directly opposite him on the other side of the orchard, he stopped shivering and peered into the darkness.

He heard a strange grunting noise. And heavy breathing.

"Oh my goodness!" He breathed to himself. "Oh my goodness!"

He had never heard such a strange sound.

Then, to his utter amazement he saw a face. It was pale and round. It was rather squashed. To be sure - it didn't seem to have a nose. But, it was framed with black and ginger hair, and looked straight at him with huge gleaming red eyes.

"Oh my goodness! Oh my! Oh my!"

This had to be the ape-man of Tasmania, he gasped to himself, as he fumbled for his camera.

"This is it! This is actually *it!*"

He brought the camera up, and, with shaking hands, snapped off a couple of shots.

Flash! Flash!

"Time to retreat," Michael's father said.

Making a louder kind of grunt, which sounded more like a kangaroo choking on a carrot, his father crawled quickly away out of the bushes.

Taking Michael's hand, they both ran for the house.

Under the apple tree Gungabum sat frozen to the spot. The yeti had obviously roared in fright. He hoped it wasn't going to attack. Thy were immensely powerful, he suddenly remembered.

However, minutes went by. Nothing happened.

Somewhat relieved, Gungabum gingerly eased himself upright. Clutching the precious camera to his chest he made his way back to the house. Every step he became more and more excited.

This was the biggest moment of his life. What a story it would be. How jealous his colleagues were going to be.

What a paper he would write.

He! Gungabum!

The apple grower's family, waiting for him at the house, were sitting in a relaxed fashion in the kitchen when Gungabum entered.

" Come in, mate," said Michael's father. "Have a cup of hot cocoa. It must be cold sitting out there."

"No time for that," cried Gungabum, slinging his binoculars on the kitchen table, "I've got photos here. I've seen it. It was actually out there. Just yards away from me. I took photos!"

Fumbling with his camera, he pressed some buttons and held it up.

"Look!" He said excitedly. "Look there it is. They have come out all right. I can't wait to get the prints so I can examine them properly."

"Let's have a look," said Michael's father. He examined the small screen where the picture on the digital camera was displayed. "Amazing!" He said.

"Oh yes!" Exclaimed Gungabum. "More than amazing. This is the find of the century. This is huge!"

"It's rather blurred, don't you think."

"Oh, don't worry about that," said Gungabum. "I'll get my lab on to it. When these photos are printed, you can be sure they'll be enhanced by my most modern digital software. You will be able to see every detail!"

"Hmm!," murmured Michael's father. "How fascinating! Though, I rather hope *not!*"

"Every detail," Gungabum repeated. "I am an expert at this."

"I am sure you are."

"This is going to make me, you know. This is going to put me on the map. It might put you on the map, as well, my dear fellow. You can forget about your apples."

"Oh dear!"

"Don't be like that. Think *tourism*! Everyone will be coming here."

"My God, I do hope not!"

"Why not! You know what this is, of course? The wild ape-man! The yeti! Big Foot! The missing link between them and us. What else can it be?"

"I'm sure I can't imagine." Replied Michael's father.

Just then, an unnaturally soft voice said:

"It's the abominable hairy man of Tasmania."

Everyone looked up. Where had this voice come from… seemingly out of nowhere?

Yes! You have guessed it. It was Michael who had spoken.

There was a stunned silence.

Everyone looked at the boy who had not uttered a word for over a year.

Michael said again: "It's the abominable hairy man of Tasmania."

Then he smiled. It was as if the sun had come out behind impenetrable clouds.

Suddenly, tears were rolling down his face which seemed so peculiar because he was laughing and crying at the same time.

He sat huddled on his chair, his arms around himself, rocking back and forth, alternatively laughing and crying.

Then, unwrapping his arms, he banged his hands hard on the kitchen table, making everybody jump and making the china rattle. Cocoa spilled everywhere and Gungabum's binoculars jumped high in the air.

His mother put her hand up to her mouth in amazement, unsure whether to laugh or cry. She was soon searching for a tissue.

His father, after a brief moment of shocked surprise, also began to shake with laughter. He was soon making great guffaws, holding his sides for all he was worth. Tears began streaming down his face into his beard.

Gungabum looked peeved.

His face took on a darker look.

"What is the meaning of this?" He shouted.

Bewildered, he looked on as the apple grower's family started hugging one another. Had the family all gone mad?

And, why was Michael the special focus of all this attention?

Had not *he*, Gungabum, discovered the yeti of Tasmania?

Michael was now in his father's arms, sobbing, his whole body trembling, his fingers entangled in a soft black beard.

But, try as he might, the apple farmer couldn't stop shaking with laughter.

"What's so funny? Professor Gungabum cried out. "What are you all laughing about. "This is a big day for me, you know!"

"It certainly is," replied Michael's father, choking back another spasm of laughter about to overwhelm him, wiping away a tear.

"It's a big day all right, mate! And we have you to thank for it."

4

THE CUBBY

There was no suitable tree in their garden for a cubby house, so Peter and Jill built their cubby in a marri tree at the back of their home, in the forest.

Old timers said that this part of the forest had once been an aboriginal burial place, the bodies being wrapped in bark and placed in the branches of the trees, allowing nature, and the wind and the rain, to do its work.

Today, there were no longer any bodies or pieces of bark left, and no bones to be seen.

Jill and Peter were not afraid of these old stories. It was just the place to build a cubby

Their special tree was an old marri (a red gum) with a knobbly trunk. Its branches were strong and thick, and spread invitingly. Just right for the planks of a cubby.

Their father helped them make it. It was not a grand affair but Jill and Peter thought it was marvellous.

Getting up to it was a bit of a scramble but it wasn't too difficult if you were small and agile.

Anyway, wasn't that the whole point of having a cubby in a tree? Difficult to see amongst the gum leaves. Difficult to climb up to. It wasn't just for anyone!

For coming down, they used a knotted rope which was tied to a strong branch.

When in residence they kept the rope curled on a branch nearby. Jill and Peter felt as if they were in their very own castle, with a drawbridge which could they pull up after them.

Going down, of course, was much easier than going up. All you had to do was hold on to the rope and shimmy down. Nimble as could be. Nothing could be simpler.

The cubby house was their very own secret place. Well, not completely secret - their parents knew about it, of course. But, at least it was secret to everyone else.

Jill and Peter were twins - not identical twins because Peter was a boy and Jill, a girl; but twins, all the same. They were the best of friends and did everything together.

In their tree house they looked down upon the world and its lesser mortals. They engaged in great schemes, and splendid games. They munched on sweets they had bought with their pocket money, or biscuits they had wangled out of their mother. They played at *house,* made plans, and giggled a lot.

They both had wonderful imaginations.

Now, it so happened that their cubby being close

to their orchard, their father had asked - if it wasn't too much trouble to ask - if they would please take an interest in the world below them.

It was all to do with the pesky parrots.

The parrots came for only one reason: to raid the orchard.

The squawky creatures savagely attacked the apricots, even before they were ripe, and, as for the almond trees, they could strip a tree of every single almond in no time at all.

"Please!" Asked their father. "Shoot at them with your catapults. Don't kill them. Just scare them away."

When hit by a little round stone or a honky nut the parrots gave a squawk and flapped off at great speed, screeching out their alarm across the valley.

Jill and Peter kept their catapults in the cubby house. They hung them from a small branch, ready for use against the parrots. They collected small stones from a stream in the valley, keeping them handy in a rusty old tin, and, of course, there were plenty of honky nuts on the ground under the gum tree.

It was fun shooting at the parrots.

It also made them feel useful.

They were repelling invaders and guarding the home.

As you can imagine, the green parrots weren't deterred for long. They kept returning to the delicious fruit so tantalisingly close to the forest.

Again and again, Jill and Peter peppered them with small stones and honky nuts until they flew away. It was a great game.

So, you won't be surprised when I tell you that both Jill and Peter became experts at shooting with their catapults. After a while, they could hit a parrot first go, every time.

Their father was very pleased.

"Those green parrots are very beautiful to look at, but they are great robbers," he said. "Thanks to you, we are going to have some fruit this year!"

Jill and Peter became expert at looking out for these robbers of the green winged variety who had little, beady, black eyes and razor sharp beaks.

Sitting in the old marri tree in their cubby at night, they could see the lights of the city twinkling in the distance. The lights of the city were a magnificent sight. Like a sea of coloured stars.

In the daytime you could see the pale grey fingers of the skyscrapers far away in the distance.

In the warm early summer evenings before bedtime, after the molten sun had vanished beneath the ocean and the orange glow in the sky had turned to a deep mauve with a thin ruby line on the horizon, Peter and Jill sat in their cubby in the old gum tree, being very still, quietly watching the night fall around them.

It was special feeling being there at night, while their parents were watching television or entertaining friends.

Sometimes a kangaroo would go thumping past, or a ghostly owl would come and perch on a branch nearby, or the friendly possum which lived nearby would arrive to sample the biscuits they had ready for it.

The children sat very still whilst the possum held the food in its paws. Unafraid, it gazed at them with huge round eyes, nibbling at the biscuit crumb like a tiny person.

Sometimes they would tell each other ghost stories - or make up stories, imagining the coloured lights below them to be space ships from another world.

Occasionally, they would think of the old ones, the first Australians, who, long ago had lived here in the hills - whose bones had once lain here in the trees - maybe, in the very tree they were sitting in. This made them shiver.

The stillness and the silence of the night surrounded them like a familiar warm cloak. You could hear the slightest thing. The whole forest, in its silence, at night, became more than just individual trees and bushes. It became a whole living thing. You could hear it breathing, smell its scent and feel its heart.

Sitting there at night, in the dark, by themselves, was just very special.

Now, it so happened, that at school that week Peter had been given a skeleton suit as a Halloween costume.

Halloween night, as you may know, is the night when some people dress up as witches and werewolves and other scary things, and carry around pumpkins as lanterns and go to fancy dress parties. Ages ago, people used to believe in witches and werewolves. Now, it is just an excuse for a bit of fun.

Peter's class at school were going to put on a play for Halloween and Peter had been given a skeleton suit to wear.

So, let me explain to you what a skeleton suit is.

Imagine a costume of black material which covers you from head to toe, having just holes for your eyes. Now, paint a skeleton on the front of this black costume of yours with luminous white paint - and you have a skeleton suit.

Luminous paint is a special paint that glows in the dark.

The skeleton painted on Peter's costume covered the whole of his suit. His head was painted in the perfect replica of a human skull, the rest of his body being painted in a spooky outline of bones, going right down to the bottom of his skeletal toes.

It was painted in luminous white paint so that in the

dark all you would see would be the ghostly outline of a skeleton. Nothing but bones. Just bones!

Very weird!

Great fun!

That very afternoon, their mother had finished altering the costume to fit Peter. It fitted him beautifully.

In the daytime it made him look a bit like Spiderman, except that it wasn't a spider's web painted on his costume. It was a full-size bony skeleton.

He couldn't wait for it to get dark.

It so happened their parents had been invited to have drinks with friends nearby. They would be back soon after dark, they said.

"We won't be very long."

Then as an afterthought, his father said jokingly. "Don't let anyone steal the family silver!"

They watched some television.

Peter kept looking out of the window to see if it was dark enough to find out what his skeleton suit looked like in the dark.

It soon began to get dark.

"Let's go to the cubby," suggested Peter. "It will be even darker in the forest."

"OK," said Jill. "Let's get some biscuits for possum."

Off they both went to the red gum tree. Climbing up to their cubby, they sat very quietly so as not to frighten the possum who might visit them only if they kept perfectly still.

It was a dark night. There was no moon, and the twinkling lights of Perth were far away, subdued by an evening mist.

"Oh," gasped Jill. "I can't see you at all, Peter. You look like a horrible skeleton."

"Ssh!" Said Peter. "You will frighten possum!"

"You mean, *you* will frighten possum," whispered his

sister. "You're skeleton is glowing a greenish-white. It looks horrible!"

"Oh, good!" Said Peter. "That is what it is meant to do. It's the luminous paint."

"Well, it's pretty ghastly."

"Great!"

"The possum won't come. It will be totally scared."

Peter smiled to himself in the dark. The more ghastly the better.

Just then they heard footsteps. A twig snapped. They smelt cigarette smoke.

"Sssh!" Whispered Jill. "Someone's coming."

Below them, in the dark, right beneath the tree, they heard a thump as if someone had dropped something heavy on the ground. Two men in rough voices began talking.

"I reckon we've done the best ones." A voice growled.

Peter and Jill could hear every word. They hardly dared to breathe. They sat frozen in silence.

"How about doing this house at the back, here?" A gruff voice replied. "Them people sure to be out. No lights on."

"You reckon?"

"Yeah, mate."

"Yeah, OK. Anything you say, mate."

"We'll leave the loot under this here tree. It'll keep. We do this last place, then come back here and share it out, OK. Then we scarper!"

"Right, mate."

"Oh my," whispered Peter in Jill's ear. "They are burglars. What do we do?"

"Nothing," breathed back Jill into his ear. "Wait till they go away and then call the police."

"We can't do that. They are going to rob our house."

"We can't do anything else."

Peter came to a decision.

"I think we can," he whispered. "Get ready to shake the tin of stones. Make it rattle! Like old bones! We'll give them the fright of their lives."

Suddenly, Peter stood up. Standing at the edge of the cubby house, he began swaying back and forth, holding out his arms and moaning.

The two men below the tree yelled an oath and sprang apart.

They looked above them and beheld an incredible sight.

A skeleton had risen from the dead, no less, from the branches of the tree. It was gleaming and glowing with an unearthly light. It moaned and swayed back and forth. Its arms were pointing straight at them.

They could hear its bones shaking in a ghastly rattle.

It was too much!

Arrrgh!

The men gave a cry and both fell to the ground paralysed with fright, shaking and sobbing.

"It's the ancestors," one of them sobbed. "We done wrong!"

"We goin' to die!"

"Sorry! Sorry!" They both moaned.

Both men were curled up on the ground, quite beyond themselves with fright, shaking and crying out as if they were in the throes of a dreadful fever.

Peter stopped moaning and swaying around for a moment.

Here was a pickle. He couldn't keep up this act for ever.

"They've got to go," he whispered to Jill. "Get the catapults!"

They reached for their catapults.

Jill knew exactly what Peter intended. In fact, she was an even better shot than he was.

She passed a stone to Peter. She had already loaded hers to fire.

Peter stood up, holding on to his catapult, easing the small stone into the leather pouch. The night was now pitch black.

The men on the ground gave another horrified glance upwards. All they saw in the black night above them was, once again, a hideous skeleton rising from the dead in the old gum tree. It's unearthly, greenish, glow was awesome.

The two men let out a miserable wail.

They couldn't move. Their legs were like jelly.

Peter took a deep breath, then bellowed out in a voice as deep as he could muster:

"Go! Go from this place and return no more! Be gone!"

Then Jill and Peter let fly with their catapults.

Jill got a shot in somewhere, because the burglar gave a great yelp. It was dark so it was impossible to see exactly where the stone had landed.

Peter also scored a direct hit with his first stone, for the second burglar gave a shriek.

"Run!" The robber shrieked. "Run for your life!"

And this they both did.

Yelling and shrieking, they stumbled off as fast as their wobbly legs could carry them, pursued by stinging stones.

Far off, in the distance, they could still be heard blundering and crashing about in the black depth of the forest as they fled for their lives.

Eventually all was silent.

"They've gone." Jill said.

"Thank goodness for that," replied Peter.

"Do you think it's all right to get down?"

"Probably is. I am shaking all over."

"We can phone Mum and Dad from the house."

They shimmied down the rope.

Jill took out her torch and shone it on the ground. Two big plastic bin liners lay there, bulging with stolen things.

"They've left their sacks behind. Their loot!"

"We'd better take it back to the house." Said Peter. " You grab one, I'll take the other."

They started back to their house, dragging the bags of stolen property behind them. "You know what," Jill said, "We can have a Halloween street party, so everyone can come and sort out what's theirs!"

"What a good idea. I can wear my suit and scare everyone to bits."

"We have done our good deed for the day, anyway," said Jill.

"Yes, Dad will be pleased," said Peter. "Do you know, Jill, I do believe we have just saved the family silver."

5

AUNTIE MAY'S DOLLAR

Whenever Auntie May came to stay the feeling in the house seem to go all weird.

You couldn't really put your finger on it, because she was really quite a nice person, but, all the same, there was *something* that did something to the usual, nice, easy feeling in the house.

Auntie May was Dad's sister.

She lived in Parramatta in the eastern states and came to stay for a few days every year - not at Christmas because she was religious and did church things with her friends in Sydney over Christmas.

This was a good thing because Christmas was always such a jolly time for us.

The problem with Auntie May was that she had a

fixation about money. She was always talking about it - in some fashion or other.

Who, for instance, had how much. Or, what they were planning to do with it. Or, shouldn't do with it. Or, how terrible the stock exchange was. Or, how the banks were ripping everyone off.

It went on and on.

Her favourite theme was that money was the root of all evil and if you had too much of it, it would make you suffer in the end, and - and this was the real bummer - if you had heaps and heaps of it, you had no hope of going to heaven when you died.

I don't know if this is true or not, but I do know that all this obsession with money wasn't making *her* very happy.

My own view is that happy people on earth go to heaven: and, unhappy people are still unhappy - even after they've died until they decide to be happy, that is. So, that's pretty simple, isn't it.

My name is Julie, by the way. I am thirteen. I have also worked out for myself that you can't be happy if, all the time, you keep thinking about things that make you unhappy.

I would have thought anyone who was as church mad as Auntie May was, could have seen that. But apparently not!

Every Christmas Auntie May sent us a huge parcel. Inside, all our presents were neatly individually wrapped and labelled, so everyone knew which present went to which person. It was all very well organised. And, despite what I have said about her money thing, she was very generous. Her presents were great!

You would never have known she had this thing about money. But she did.

I think she had secret obsessions about other things, too. But, if she did she was good at keeping them secret.

Because, when she smiled, it always seemed a bit artificial, as if she was hiding something - like her smile had been painted on her face by something else going on in her brain.

She smiled a lot.

She was always smiling. .

This is what made me think she had other secrets. It was a shame because she had quite a pretty face. It might even have been beautiful, more soft and glowing, like Jana's, perhaps.

Now, this story really has a lot to do, I suppose, with Jana - my mother's friend, who lives close by. Jana often drops in for a chat and a cup of tea, and, of course, some of Mum's wonderful buttered scones - made with real butter, mind you, not that margarine stuff.

Jana is into crystals and incense, and yoga and meditation. She believes in reincarnation - which, she says, is about returning many times to earth in a different body until you have learnt that you can be happy on earth exactly the same as you can be happy in heaven!

She is definitely a wise woman. I like her. In fact, I think she is wonderful. She is always as poor as a church mouse. But, her smile lights up the house and she is great fun to be with.

I am not sure if crystals and incense are for me, but yoga seems very good for my mother; it keeps her trim; and, as for reincarnation perhaps it makes a lot of sense when you come to think about it.

After all, what is the purpose in being here, if we are not learning something.

And, I would have thought, learning how to be happy is a very good thing to learn!

I thought, one day, I would like to be a wise woman like Jana.

Anyway, one day when Auntie May was staying with

us - we were all in the kitchen at the time, having afternoon tea - Jana dropped in as she often did.

She had brought some flowers from her garden and a box of eggs. Wonderful big eggs they were. Each of her hens had a name (which I have now forgotten) but I do remember she had a cock called Winston. He was a huge shiny red rooster. We could hear him crowing from our house every morning.

I do believe my mother had told Jana about Auntie May but it was the first time they had met face to face.

I could see that, for some reason, Auntie May was very uncomfortable around Jana. Her smile was more fixed than ever.

Of course, inevitably, the subject got round to money.

Auntie May was complaining that some big industrialists were controlling the world banks, and the worlds banks were controlling the economy, and everyone was going down the tube.

"What can you do about it?" asked Jana, buttering another scone, smiling sweetly.

"Oh, that's not up to me," said Auntie May. "I just know what has to be done."

Oh, yes, what is that?"

"They should give away their money, of course. Make sure everyone has enough. Then there would be no more poor people in the world."

Auntie May sat back in her chair, looking very satisfied. Surely, no one could object to that!

But Jana merely wrinkled up her nose which reminded me of that witch on television who does the same thing just before she works her magic: "Would that make *you* happy?"

Auntie May wiped her thin lips with a napkin. "Of course it would!"

Jana gazed off into the distance.

Auntie May crunched her napkin into a ball and threw it on to the table. I could see she was starting to get angry but trying hard not to show it. Her fixed smile was beginning to twitch at the edges of her face.

I could also sense Mother was starting to get concerned. She didn't want bad feelings over her buttered scones. Afternoon tea was a time for harmony and light banter, not deep and meaningful confrontations where hidden feelings could emerge and escalate into unpleasantness.

Auntie May sat stiffly. She said in a clipped and icy voice: "I'm already a happy person. Thank you."

"Good," said Jana. She unconcernedly helped herself to another scone. I passed her the strawberry jam. The jam was also home-made. It was absolutely delicious.

"Well," continued Jana, who, surprisingly, wasn't yet finished with the subject. "That's all right, then. It is the greatest thing you can do for the world. Just being happy."

Auntie May looked nonplussed. She wasn't sure of this was a compliment or not. Was she being praised or was she being got at?

She decided against taking issue with it, anyway; but did so with a distinctly unhappy expression on her face.

Mother decided to intervene. "How are your chickens behaving?" She asked Jana, valiantly trying to change the subject. She turned to Auntie May. "Jana has names for all her hens, you know. She lets them wander around her garden and plays music to them."

Jana smiled. "I try to keep my hens happy."

"That's nice," said Auntie May who lived in an apartment in Parramatta and hadn't been close to a hen for more years than you could poke a stick at.

"My girls have simple needs." said Jana. "They just get on with the business of being themselves, and, of course, rewarding me with beautiful eggs. They know I love them."

"If everyone was like that the world would be a happier place," said Auntie May primly.

"Indeed," said Jana, "Love is everything."

"Love can't quite be everything. What about the devil?" said Auntie May. She made an ugly grimace.

"Oh him!" said Jana dismissively, waving her napkin in the air. "That's just an old wives tale to frighten people into behaving the way others think they should. There's no such thing. It's all a load of mediaeval baloney. Love is everything. Anything else is man made: thought up by human beings for some reason or other. Usually to keep others under control. To stop them being happy!"

Auntie May looked shocked. She went quite white.

"How can you say that," she stuttered. "That's heresy. That's saying there's no God."

"No!" Said Jana. "It's saying there's no devil."

"Not everything is love. What about money! Money can't be love! Money is definitely of the devil!" She looked triumphant.

I could almost hear Mother groan inside. Oh, no, not back to money again!

"Whatever you want to believe, you believe," said Jana calmly.

"I am a member of the church," said Auntie May stoutly. "I don't agree that money is love. I don't believe anyone could possibly think that."

Jana just gave a small smile. "Maybe you will find out one day." She twitched her nose back and forth, looking more like Samantha - you know, that witch on television - than ever. "Maybe I'll send you some help."

Jana turned to Mum, wiping butter off her lips: "You are truly the best scone maker in the world, my dear, but I have to go now. Thank you so much for tea. We'll catch up."

Then she turned to Auntie May. "It has been a pleasure. Are you staying long?"

"Another week," said Auntie May rather gruffly. "I have to be back in Sydney for Easter."

Jana nodded. "Good plan," she said rather vaguely. "Good plan."

Next morning, Auntie May didn't put in an appearance for breakfast, but I went to her room anyway with a cup of tea. She always had a cup of green tea with lemon in it, without sugar, every morning before breakfast. It was her regular thing.

She wasn't in her room and she wasn't in the bathroom. I wondered where she could be.

Her bed had been slept in. That was obvious. Her pillow had a dent in it.

Then, when I looked again, I saw, sitting right in the middle of it, just exactly where her head had been, a shiny bright gold dollar coin.

I kind of idly picked it up and looked at it. It was so shiny it looked brand new.

But, glancing at the date on the coin, I was surprised to see that it had been minted in the very year Auntie May was born. What a strange coincidence. Or, was it?

I didn't think much of it at the time. I popped it in my pocket, thinking to show it to her at breakfast.

I said to myself, "It's money. She's sure to find it interesting".

Then, another thought occurred to me: maybe she already knew. Maybe, it was her lucky dollar.

I was about to put it back, when I heard the bathroom door open.

And, just like me, I promptly forgot all about it. I was now involved in that mad rush that our house undergoes every morning.

Our bathroom was a real bottleneck. You had to jump in when you could.

However, Auntie May didn't turn up all day.

We weren't particularly concerned because she often took off by herself to go on long walks, especially as we lived by the beach.

Many times she would drop in at a beach cafe and have croissants and coffee, not getting back till lunch.

Today, though, she hadn't told anyone where she was going.

Mother said she had probably got up very early and didn't want to wake us.

I wondered about that, because Auntie May was the sort of person who pretty well planned out everything in advance, knew what everyone was doing or was going to do. She was a stickler for order and having everything just so.

It wasn't like her not to say where she was going.

I caught the bus into town to go to my dance class and, unthinkingly paid for it with the shiny dollar. At the last moment, as it was dropping down the chute into the money box, I realised it was Auntie May's shiny dollar. But, too late. It had gone.

The last thing - the very last thing - I ever would have guessed, was that it was me who had dropped *Auntie May* down the chute!

I don't want to jump ahead too far in this story, except to say: that a week later, the day before Auntie May was to fly back to Sydney, she and I - just the two of us - were sitting in the garden, listening to the early morning kookaburras and the melodious warbling of the magpies, Auntie May with her lemon tea, and me warming my hands round my cup of Milo, my flute on the bench next to me. It was then that she told me what had happened.

It was a strange story.

First, though, let me tell you: after she returned, she wouldn't say a word to anyone of where she'd been or what she'd been up to. Mother still held to the belief she had been on a walk. Jana said she had been on a journey.

And, in a way, I suppose she had.

She certainly surprised us that night, the way she materialised out of nowhere. None of us had seen her return to the house. We all thought she was still out walking. Father had been getting worried, He had been on the point of phoning the police.

Then, she suddenly appeared from out of her room, astonishing me because I had only been in there moments before and I hadn't seen her. Her demeanour was rather serious She didn't wish anyone good evening which was her usual thing, but made a great fuss over Pip, our dog, who seemed unusually delighted to see her. She nodded to everyone, pulled back her chair and sat quietly down, her hands folded calmly under the table as demurely as a nun.

Let me tell you, this was *so* unusual; because, when she usually sat at the table she would re-arrange the cutlery, the napkin, the sauce bottle, or whatever was close by, to her liking, her fingers all over the place. But, tonight, here she was sitting as calmly as could be - almost daring me, I thought wickedly, to ask if she was quite certain her knife and fork were straight enough.

Yes, it was plain to all of us. We couldn't help but notice that *something* had happened to Auntie May. She seemed that night...well, different. Her face was softer. Her eyes were softer. She was sort of softer all over.

And, she had stopped smiling.

For the first time, her smile, when she did smile, seemed to be a proper smile. In fact, she had stopped that irritating habit of hers of smiling all the time, even when there was nothing to smile about.

Later, when Auntie May had retired to her room earlier than usual, I asked Dad if he knew where she'd been all day? Dad shook his head and gave me a wink and a nudge, saying Auntie May must have met someone on her walk.

I was wondering how long the soft glow would last.

I am happy to tell you it lasted for ever.

After that walk of hers - which I now know, of course, wasn't really a walk, but a weird adventure - she was a vastly changed person.

It wasn't due to anyone she had met. It was something else entirely.

Let me tell you her strange - her ultra strange - story, in her own words.

It is worth listening to because, I for one, have never heard anything so strange.

My name is May. I am not at home. I am staying with my brother and his family in Golden Bay near Perth. I am lying in bed, dawn is breaking. The kookaburras woke me and the magpies are warbling outside my window. Very irritating really. Why can't they be quiet like everyone else first thing in the morning.

I am hoping my niece, Julie, won't take it into her head to practice her flute in the garden, either. She is a clever girl, by all accounts, but has the irritating habit of giving me half an hour of Greensleeves first thing in the morning outside my window, then bursting into my room with a cup of tea.

As if I can't get my own tea!

However, she does, at least, know how I like it. I smile at the dear girl and try hard not to be irritated.

I always get up early. I do like to lie in bed before getting up, thinking about all the things I'm going to do, today. But, I never lounge around in bed all day like some people do. No way! Idle hands do the devil's work, father always used to say, and I agree!

Suddenly, I have a brief picture in my head of

Jana - the strange woman who came to afternoon tea yesterday. What an impossible woman. I can't think why my brother's family like her. She's got some hard truths coming her way one day...yes, I am sure about that!

I quickly put her out of my mind.

I am lying there composing myself for the day, thinking I might go for a brisk walk along the beach, when all of a sudden I seem to nod off again.

Very unlike me.

I wake up and find I can't move. That's right. I can't move a muscle.

Here I am, perfectly awake, feeling as fresh as a daisy, as good as new, but I can't move. I look down at myself and have the shock of my life.

I have turned into a shiny dollar coin.

I am round and hard, and coloured gold. I have a picture of kangaroo on one side of me, and on the other side a woman with something on her head. Probably a crown. I don't know. Lordy, it's got to be the Queen! There is also writing around my edges but I can't read what it says because my eyes, being on each side of the coin - one in the middle of the kangaroo and the other in the middle of the smart looking woman with the crown on her head - don't reach that far.

I am getting cross-eyed.

All of a sudden, my much too-cheerful niece comes in with my morning cuppa - she often puts in too much lemon; once, putting in grapefruit by mistake - oh, what a horror that was! But she doesn't see me.

At least, she doesn't see the real me, she just sees the dollar coin that I have now become. She twirls me round and round in the palm of her hand. I get quite dizzy. I think I might be sick.

Then the stupid girl puts me in the pocket of her dressing gown.

Well! I ask you.

Her dressing gown pocket smells of Minties, and rubber bands. Ugh!

There is a dim light showing through the material of the pocket. I feel lost and utterly helpless. What has become of me!

I think I must have passed out for a while because my next sensation is of Julie running. I can hear her panting. I am jiggling up and down in a pocket of her jeans, quite helpless to do anything but jiggle. I hear a bus pull up. She climbs on board.

Next, I'm tumbling down a metal tube on to a pile of coins. I am on a bus, in a cash box. All the other coins are horrid and dirty. They smell of cigarette smoke, of perfumed handbags, and toilet cleaner - or is it soap powder? Some are sticky with marmalade and chewing gum. Yuk!

At least, my niece is happy she has caught the bus. That is something!

I can hear her talking happily to a friend about how she nearly missed it because of me and my lemon tea, and how I wasn't there.

How girls do natter on!

The next think I know is the bus driver is scooping me out of the cash box and I am being rolled up in a paper tube alongside nineteen other dollar coins. I am put in a dark place with other rolled up tubes of coins; and taken somewhere, in one of those big solid security vans. I think it is to a bank.

All of us rolls are rolled up together and placed in a safe. I hear the door of the safe open with a beeping noise, then close with a solid *wumph!*

What is happening to me. I don't like being forced in this close to my fellow coins. I find it hard to breathe. It is suffocating. I feel humiliated.

I am glad to say, it doesn't last long.

Suddenly, there is a bright light. With other coins I am broken out of the paper tube and put in a drawer. A bank teller gives me as change to an old woman who smells of moth balls. She is small and upright and walks with a stick.

She is very happy to have me.

Good, I think. But, what now?

Just then, I hear running feet. A handbag snatcher grabs the old woman's purse out of her hand.

I am in the purse. I hear her scream. There is shouting, more running feet.

There is no more smell of mothballs; now, I am smelling engine oil. I hear the roar of a motorbike starting up. I smell burning rubber, and we are rushing somewhere like the wind.

The robber is laughing.

He is a happy man, I think. He has done a bad thing. But, at least he is happy.

Good or bad, everyone is doing what they want to do, it seems - using me to do it!

I wonder what is happening here? Everyone is happy to have me! Happy using me!

For a while, at least.

Very strange.

I am feeling distinctly uncomfortable with this idea.

Who am I? Am I *me* or am I money? Or, am I both? Perhaps I am both.

This is a very strange thought.

Eventually, the noise of the motorbike comes to an end. I smell beer and a loud amount of laughter and chatter, and the clink of glasses. There is cigarette smoke. It is a familiar smell. I have been in a pub before. I remember it. Years ago.

I am handed over to the man behind the bar in exchange for a cold can of fizzing beer.

The handbag snatcher is happy to have got his beer. I can hear him calling out to a mate.

The pub keeper is also glad to have me.

"The money is rolling in today," I hear him saying happily to his wife.

Everyone, it seems, is happy today except for me.

Just then, a Salvation Army man comes in the door of the pub shaking his tin.

The pub keeper sweeps me off the wet counter - I am now smelling of beer, ugh! He drops me in the tin, being shaken up and down in front of his nose. He wants to set a good example in front of his customers.

"A nice new one," he says. "Bright and shiny."

"Good on yer, mate," the Salvo says.

He is happy to have got such a nice bright shiny coin in his tin. Me!

But I am not.

For the next few hours I am being shaken up and down like a mad thing, up and down, up and down, on and on, being shaken to bits and nearly deafened by the noise of the infernal rattling. Shake! Shake! Rattle ! Rattle!

"Give to the Salvos." He shouts. "A coin for the Salvos!"

Can you imagine it! It was indescribably horrid.

I soon felt terribly sick, but, as I had no stomach to be sick from, I couldn't be. It was small consolation.

At last, however, the dreadful shaking and rattling came to an end, and I was thrown on to a table with a great heap of other coins to be counted.

When the Salvation Army man came to me he picked me up to examine me and gave a gasp.

"Hey!" he yelled to a woman who was also sorting coins at the next table. "Have a gander at this."

"What are you goin' on about, now," grumbled a fat

woman who smelt of boiled cabbage smothered by eau de cologne.

"Here! I collect coins, see. I am always looking for a rare one. This one must be very rare. It's got a date on it I never heard of. No dollar coin should have this date. None was minted that year. Or, if they was, it was only a handful. In good nick, too".

"You mean it could be worth something," the woman said. She was starting to sound happy.

"Oh, yes, it could be worth a bob or two. Probably a fair bit!"

Oh, my!" the woman said. "Captain will be happy."

"I will put it aside for now," the man said. "I will check it out later. I've got a book on coins at home, the dates an' all, and what they're worth."

He sounded a happy man.

Which, got me to thinking: was he happy because of me - or because I was money?

It was rather a depressing thought. But I came to the conclusion it was not because of me.

The man wrapped me in his handkerchief which smelled of...oh dear, I don't think I can tell you what it smelt of...it was horrible. All gummy and sticky. He had a cold, you see, and he had been blowing his nose a lot.

He was a rather absent minded old fellow, though, and the very next time he sneezed - as he was walking home - he unthinkingly pulled out his handkerchief and off I went rolling down the road. He didn't even know I had gone.

The next thing I heard was a child crying. She was being pulled along by the arm by a thin young woman who looked as she could do with a good nourishing meal.

The child found me, picked me up and stopped crying. She showed me proudly to her thin young mother who was very pleased to see me. "We will go and get a bun," she said to her daughter. They both went off happily, me being clutched tightly in her daughter's tiny warm hand.

They were laughing together.

What a small thing, I am thinking, it is to make people happy. Just one small coin.

I am carried to a corner deli and exchanged for a bun. The deli owner is pleased to see me. He hasn't been too happy recently, ever since the new supermarket store opened nearby.

I don't like him much. He has a greasy, seedy, appearance. But, all the same, my personal likes and dislikes don't come into it. I am money. He is happy to have me.

I am thinking, nice or nasty, good or bad, rich or poor, money treats everyone the same way.

And, money makes people happy. At least, they are happy to have it. It is a fact. I have seen it with my own eyes.

Then I have a strange thought: maybe money *loves* everybody?

Well, that's a bit of a stretch!

Don't be silly, May, I say to myself.

Anyway, one thing I can be sure of: money doesn't have favourites. More or less, treats everybody the same - and everybody is happy to have it.

What remarkable stuff it is! Well, I mean…now, what I am thinking is: if you met a person like that *you'd call him a saint*. Of course, you would. Surely, only someone close to God would be so impartially wonderful.

I am deep in thought, falling into bottomless pit of astonishing ideas, lost to my predicament, my mind beginning to spin in technicolour - I can feel I'm losing it - when, to my amazement, Julie, my niece, arrives. She dashes breathlessly into the deli, clutching her dancing shoes. She buys a packet of Minties. I am given to her as change. She is in a hurry.

Why are teenagers always in a hurry!

She barely looks down at the coin in her hand, yet recognizes it and gives a whoop of joy.

She is so happy to see me.

"Whassa matter, then?" says the shop keeper. "Never had Minties before?"

"This is the coin I lost this morning," shouts Julie, running from the shop. "I've got to get it back. It doesn't belong to me."

So, Julie dear - good girl that you are - you kindly put me back where you found me, on my pillow, where I soon woke up and found myself to be myself again.

And thank goodness for that, too, I must say.

It all seemed like a dream, but the vividest dream I ever did have. So vivid, in fact, that I knew it was much more than a dream.

I think your mother's friend Jana had something to do with it.

In fact, I wouldn't be surprised if she didn't have *everything* to do with it. She is a strange woman, that one. With that twitchy nose of hers.

You might have noticed, dear Julie - and I know that you have, you were always the clever one - that I have become a different person. Something has changed in me. I am seeing things in a different way.

I now realize, that what I believed would make me happy has not been making me happy, and everything I have been busy believing was *wrong* with the world has some value in it that I never suspected. Nothing is how I imagined it to be.

In fact, it seems, all this time I have had my life back to front.

It has knocked me for six, I can tell you.

All the years I have been coming to stay with you,

I must have been dreadfully boring, I am sure. Was I such a terrible pain to be around? Do forgive me for that, Julie.

Next time I come to stay with you, Julie dear, I would like to meet your mother's friend again. Do you think you could arrange that for me? I am sure we will have a lot to talk about.

Aren't the magpies singing beautifully this morning. Will you play your flute for me before I leave today.

6

GRANDMA'S PUTTER

Jason was just ten years old when he first picked up a golf club.

He had thought, perhaps, he would like to be a policeman and live in New Zealand because he liked mountains. But, the very day he picked up a golf club he forgot about New Zealand and mountains - or being a policeman.

He knew golf was for him.

He would be the best golfer in the world, become famous, and make lots of money.

Well, and why not! It was as good a plan as any!

The first time his father took him to a proper golf course was an exciting day for Jason. It also turned out - as I will recount - to be a rather *momentous* day.

Now, as his father was Australian he called golf clubs *sticks*. I don't know why, but Australians do. His mother was English and called them *clubs* like everyone else.

His grandma also called them *clubs*, of course, as she had learnt her golf in Scotland where golf was invented so it is said by bored shepherds using their crooks to hit stones into holes amongst the heather. But that was a long time ago.

Jason and his family now lived in southern England, not far from the city of Bournemouth. Their home overlooked the grey waters of the English channel.

"You can play with grandma's old sticks," his father said. "They are smaller than mine. They'll suit you better. Don't mind if they look old, they still play fine."

Jason looked at grandma's old clubs dubiously.

They weren't just old. They were positively ancient. And their shafts were not shiny bright steel shafts but made of wood.

"They look awfully old," said Jason.

"Just to start you off," said his father, seeing Jason's expression.

"No one plays with wooden clubs," Jason said.

"Your grandma did and she was a champion putter. Better than anyone I ever knew. Once she was on the green she only ever needed one shot. That's how she got her nickname, dead-eye Di."

Now, the Studland Golf Club which is by the sea and close to Bournemouth is a pretty golf course. From much of the course you can see the sea over the top of sand dunes, the first tee being next to the club house.

Today, because there was a wind blowing, members of the club who weren't playing golf were sitting inside by the windows, sipping their coffee and nibbling their hot cheesy croissants.

It was a cool fresh morning. Heavy grey clouds were scudding low over the water. The ratlines of the sail boats moored in the harbour were tinkling in the wind. Fine plumes of sand were whipping off the tops of the dunes.

"Off you go, mate," said Jason's father. "Tee up first. That's right. Have a few practice swings first, if you like. Everyone does. Don't mind the people watching. That's the idea."

Jason stuck the little red tee in the ground and placed

his shiny new golf ball on top of it. It perched up nicely off the ground. It would be easy to hit with his driver.

The wooden driver was the longest club in his grandma's old bag. It had a peculiar oblong shaped head with deep grooves scored in its face.

He had no doubt he could whack the ball with the driver however peculiar or old fashioned it was. Hadn't he been practicing for some days with a ball on a string, at home on the lawn?

Jason got himself into a good stance. His feet firmly astride and opposite the ball. He waggled the club back and forth a few times while his father looked on approvingly. Then, he gave the ball a mighty blow.

Unfortunately, instead of hitting the ball, he hit the ground in front of it with a mighty wallop. Down he came on the ground like a man chopping wood. Dust flew up. The ball didn't move. But, the head of Jason's driver did. It parted from its wooden shaft and went flying off down the fairway like a rocket. It went a considerable distance.

If it had been the ball that had flown off down the fairway it would have been a good shot - at least, a reasonable first time effort. But, alas, it was not the ball that went off like a flying missile but the head of grandma's driver.

With dismay, Jason was left clutching the broken wooden shaft.

There was an ironic, muted cheer from behind the glass windows of the club house. Members raised their cups in a toast to the unfortunate Jason.

How embarrassing. He didn't know where to look.

"Well, that's a first!" said his father. "But, don't worry about those people in the club house. They've all done worse things in their time. Pick yourself up and have another go."

"I don't have another driver," complained Jason, examining the broken stick.

"Try your number three," said his father. Your grandma swore by her number three."

Grandma's number three iron also looked ancient. Its iron head had bits of metal chewed out of its lower edge. It was dark and rusty. Its handle was bound in smooth black leather. The handle had a slippery feel to it. The leather looked old.

There was nothing for it but to have another try. Jason held the number three iron in his hands for a moment to get the feel of it. He addressed the ball again, standing firmly astride, waggling the club this way and that as he had seen all the best golfers do.

His father held his breath.

More club members had gathered behind the windows in the club house, their glasses raised half way to their lips.

Jason raised grandma's number three iron. It went up and up. Around his shoulder it went.

It came back with a mighty swing. The air went *whoosh!*

But, did Jason hit the ball?

No! He did not. The ball remained where it was. Instead, the whole golf stick went flying off into the distance. All Jason was left holding onto was a coiled strip of black leather which, having become unglued due to its age, had slipped off the wooden handle of the golf stick.

Oh, dear me! How impossibly humiliating this was!

In dismay, Jason stared down at his hands which were holding the coil of rotten black leather. Grandma's number three iron was now lying somewhere down the fairway, not far - as it happened - from the broken head of grandma's driver.

His new shiny white golf ball still sat on its new red

tee, as shiny as ever. He had already had two shots at it, had destroyed two golf clubs in the process, and it hadn't moved a millimetre.

Jason felt like crying. But he was determined not to.

He still wanted to be a famous golfer.

The ironic cheers now coming from the club house were not the kind of cheers he had imagined hearing.

"Never mind, mate," said his father. "I guess grandma's sticks are older than I thought. Perhaps we should try another day. We will find you some new sticks."

Jason, however, was made of sterner stuff.

"That's two shots I've had." He said.

"No worries!" His father said. "Well, as you're a beginner, you get some leeway. Start over!"

Jason was getting angry with himself and the whole situation.

"I am going to do grandma proud." He said to himself. If she played so well with these golf sticks, there was no reason why he couldn't, either! His grandma had loved these sticks.

In hospital, before she died, she had motioned him close: "Jason, dear." She had said. " Look after my golf clubs. Especially, the putter which is very old. Never give it away or lend it to anyone. It's rather special."

His father saw the determination on his face. "You could try her number five," he said. "She called it her *mashie*. That's the old Scottish name for a number five."

"I will try the *mashie*," said Jason. A thought came to him. "Or, maybe I could use her putter. She said her putter was special."

His father chuckled. "It was. She never missed with it. She said a strange old shepherd she'd met in Scotland gave it to her. The old fellow told her it had been made by the little people in the wild glens of Scotland, and she was never to lend it to anyone. But, if you believe that, you'll believe anything."

Jason went to pull out grandma's *mashie*, but somehow his hand went to the putter.

He had pulled the putter out of grandma's golf bag before he realized his mistake.

"Not that one," said his father. "You won't go anywhere with that. You only use a putter on the green."

"But the *mashie* has got a sloping head," Jason said. "I won't go far with that. The ball will just go high in the air. At least, the putter has got a flat head. It will go further. Won't it?"

His father shook his head.

"The putter is only for the green. Anyway, don't bother about going far, for now. Just hit the ball with the number five and hope for the best," he said. "It's true, grandma never missed with her putter, but you've got to get on the green first. Use the number five."

But, by this time, Jason was feeling obstinate.

"I am fed up with this game." he said petulantly. "Golf is a stupid game."

He glanced at the putter he was holding. Its head was unpolished brass. The shaft of the small club, unlike others in the bag, was of a darker wood and gleamed as if polished. Its handle was bound with green leather.

Despite its oddly shaped head which was flat to the line of the club and scored by three grooves, it wasn't rusty like some of the other clubs were. When given a rub the glint of brass shone through. It looked in good shape. In fact, it looked in better shape than many of the other clubs in grandma's ancient bag. Not prehistoric perhaps, but it did look old.

How old was it? He wondered. Who had made this strange club?

Examining its wooden shaft, he saw that there were letters carved into the dark polished wood. They were bitten deep into the hard wood like ancient runes.

All is blessed when all is One,
I am blessed by a hole in One.

"I wonder what they mean?"

Without thinking he started swinging the putter around to get the feel of it.

"No! No! No!" Cried his father. "Not the putter!"

But, too late. Jason had lifted the putter above his shoulder.

The putter swept down, hitting the ball smack in its centre. The little white ball flew off the tee as if it had been shot from a gun.

Down the fairway it sped. It curved way off to the right and hit the branch of a tall cypress with a great *crack.*

It spun off the fir tree and went hurtling into a nearby road where it struck the roof of a speeding car with a *clunk.*

The tiny white ball, going faster than ever, rocketed off the roof of the car with such speed that it actually overtook the car and landed back on to the fairway.

Having returned to the fairway, the ball bounced high in the air a number of times and headed for the green.

The green could be barely seen. But, there it was, in the distance, above the sand dunes, its red flag waving snappily in the wind blowing off the English channel.

The golf ball hurtled down the short clipped grass of the fairway, heading straight for the green. On to the green it went.

It crossed the silky smooth grass of the green. It was travelling more slowly now, but unerringly on and on it ran.

It made a bee line for the flag pole. It hit the flag pole with a faint tinny *clang* and dropped into the hole.

"Stone the crows!" said his father, clasping his hands to his face. "I do believe you've done a hole-in-one."

Cheers erupted from the club house.

This time they were proper cheers.

People started trickling out.

"Well, blow me down," said his father. "What did you do?"

"I just hit the ball with grandma's putter like she told me," replied Jason.

"There's something very strange about that putter," mused his father. " I always thought grandma was too lucky for her own good. Mate, you'd better keep it for the green. You can't go doing holes-in-one all the time. People will get all *thingy*!"

People being all *thingy* - whatever it was - didn't sound good to Jason.

"All right," he said, "I'll keep it for the greens in future."

"Be best. Be cheaper, too. Otherwise you'll be buying drinks all the time. The custom here is if you get a hole-in-one you buy drinks for everyone."

"I am too young to go in the bar," said Jason.

"Well, that's true," agreed his father. "It'll be me who'll be paying."

"Don't worry," said Jason. "It will be the last time I use grandma's putter off the tee. I will only use it on the greens."

He was as good as his word.

When you are next in England, go to the Studland Golf Club. Ask to see a small round plaque tucked away in a corner near the bar. It commemorates a hole-in-one made by a young boy's first shot at golf.

It says he drove off the first tee with - believe it nor not - a *putter*, and made a hole-in-one.

Some of the older members say they remember it. Others say it is a load of rubbish. A fairy tale,

You can make up your own mind.

I won't tell you this boy's - who is now a man - second name because that would be giving away his secret. But, I can tell you this: he is a famous golfer, now - just as he wanted to be.

People are puzzled that he carries in a separate pouch in his golf bag a very ancient wooden putter with a brass head and a green leather handle.

Truly, he's a wizard with that putter.

Watch him if you can. He is in most of the big tournaments. But don't ask him if you can borrow his putter.

He will say it's too old - too precious to lend out.

If you get to know him better, he will tell you it belonged to his grandma.

Over a beer at the nineteenth hole he might even tell you it was made in a fairy glen amongst the heather and ancient standing stones by the little people, somewhere deep in the highlands of old Scotland. He'll say it in such a way as to make you think he's joking.

He, probably, *won't* tell you that she never missed with it.

Or, that he has never been known to miss with it, either.

On the greens in Australia, they call him dead-eye Jay.

7

THIS IS MY SEAT

One fine sunny morning as I was strolling along the seafront at Brighton, there I was, close to its famous pier, enjoying the fresh salty air and watching the girls and boys whizzing past on their roller skates, generally having a lazy and enjoyable stroll, when I came across a clump of people in a circle yelling their heads off and carrying on like a crowd of race-goers.

But it wasn't horses they were shouting for, or boxers, or anything like that. When I poked my head over the ring of spectators, I saw to my immense surprise, two very elderly - they must have been at least eighty if they were a day - gentlemen, going at each other hammer and tongs with their walking sticks.

"What's going on?" I asked a man close to me.

"They are fighting a duel," he said.

With walking sticks?

Looking closer I saw that the two men who were going at each other with such astonishing geriatric vigour were using their walking sticks like swords. They must have been going at it for a while for they were both puffing and panting and rather red in the face

Each had a stance such as you might find in a fencing hall. One man had his left hand tucked neatly out of the way behind his bottom while the other was waving his left hand, his non-sword hand - or should I say, his non-walking stick hand - airily in the air beside him as if he was conducting a band.

Both gentlemen had a distinguished air about them. Red in the face, yes. But their faces both held determination, intelligence and the look of one time leaders of the British Empire. Having removed their coats and jackets, they were fencing in their waistcoats. Incongruously, they were both also wearing city-type bowlers - the kind of hat that went out of fashion years ago. What mystery was this?

I noticed their walking sticks were rather different. One was fighting with a cane which had a silver knob for its handle, while the other gentleman who had generous tufts of white hair sticking out from under his bowler had the conventional kind of walking stick; an ordinary looking mahogany with a curved handle.

Both were wielding their sticks - their wooden swords, if you like - with a great deal of professionalism. Neither seemed able to touch the other. Shots at the body were quickly deflected by the clash of their wooden weapons.

"One of them will score a hit soon," the man next to me muttered. "They are tiring."

"What's it all about?" I tried again.

"Soon we'll be all off to the Crown and Anchor."

"The pub?" I replied still mystified.

"Yes, the pub," he said. "We all go off and have a grand lunch and booze up."

"Why the fight?" I persevered.

"The fight? This is not a fight. Well, it's not a proper fight. It's a re-enactment, I suppose you could call it.

They do it every year here. Once a year, to see who wins - and to keep their hand in, as it were, and to keep the memory alive of when they first met."

"When they first met?" I repeated rather stupidly.

"Oh, that was a real fight, all right," he said. "That was a to-the-death fight, but they ended up good friends. Must have been all of twenty years ago.Look now!" He gesticulated excitedly. "The Commander has got him on the back foot."

Indeed, the gentleman with the fluffy white hair and the ordinary mahogany walking stick was pressing forward with a sudden renewed burst of energy while the gentleman with the silver-handled cane was falling back against the crowded circle, which began to give way before the backwardly propelled fencer.

A shout went up. "A hit! *Touche* !"

"Hurrah!"

Hands were thrown in the air. People cheered.

"That was close," the man next to me said. "Last year the Colonel won."

The two elderly protagonists were wiping their brows with towels which had materialised out of the baskets of a couple of women nearby who, I now saw, were also holding their jackets. Both men were beaming as happily as twelve year olds who had scored a winning goal. They vigorously pumped each other's hands. With their arms around each other's shoulders, they began to move off. The one who had lost shouted out, cheerfully: "To the Crown and Anchor!"

This raised another even bigger cheer.

"Come along," my new friend said. "I'll tell you all about it in the pub. It's quite a story."

So I went along with him and most of that crowd as well to the pub, and a very jolly time we had, and a very good Sunday lunch it was, too.

In between much banter and liquid refreshment

and a splendid roast lunch, he told me how this quaint custom of an annual duel with walking sticks by these two geriatric, military gentlemen, had come about - beginning all of twenty years ago.

Here is the story.

Two gentlemen were travelling down to Brighton on the London to Brighton train. Bother were retired military gentlemen, one had been a Colonel in the Army, the other a Commander in the Royal Navy. They didn't know each other; they had never met during their careers in these two quite different branches of military service.

Both were distinguished looking and both wore bowler hats as was customary in those days in the City when dressed in civilian clothes. One carried a cane with a silver knob as its handle, the other had beside him on his seat an ordinary, darkly polished, mahogany walking stick.

The gentleman with the silver headed stick was Colonel George Grant. VC. (Retired). The gentleman with the ordinary walking stick was Commander Anthony Oliver. OBE. (Retired).

Both were sitting opposite each other in the two window seats of the train. They were alone in the compartment and didn't talk to each other. After a quick glance at the other when they had first boarded the train, and a quick touch with the fingers to the brim of each bowler hat, each busied himself with the copy of his Times newspaper.

Commander Anthony Oliver, being a man of the sea, and liking fresh air, as well as liking to see where he - or his ship in his days at sea - were going, chose to sit in the seat facing the engine. Colonel George Grant,who came in a moment later - though he had been in command of a tank regiment and liked to see where his tanks were going - had to be content with sitting with his back to the engine.

After a while Commander Oliver had had enough of fresh air and smutty smoke spots hitting his face, not to mention the wind which was fast becoming a nuisance, ruffling the pages of his newspaper. He went to close the window and snapped it shut.

The Colonel looked up from his reading and humphed: "Don't want to be stuffy!"

"Excuse me?"

"I said, we don't want to be stuffy. We need air."

The Commander looked a little nonplussed. He decided to do what gentlemen do before communicating with each other.

"Let me introduce myself. Commander Anthony Oliver late of His Majesty's Royal Navy."

"Colonel George Grant, late of the First Royal Tank Regiment." The Colonel politely touched the rim of his bowler while the barest flicker of a smile touched his lips.

They shook hands.

The Commander said. "Did you want the window open? I was finding ita bit much."

"Probably was." The Colonel said briefly. He went back to his paper. The Commander stared at him for a moment, then went back to his. Obviously the discussion was finished.

Anyway, what did it matter. They would probably never see each other again. And, above all, a gentleman should be left alone to read his newspaper.

The Colonel, however, although he had his nose in his newspaper, was busy thinking to himself: "Pah! *A seaweed wallah!*"

You need to understand that in those days the Army didn't have a lot of time for Navy men and the Navy, as a result, didn't have much time for Army *flat foots* - as they called them. Politely, it was called inter-service rivalry.

Just then the train stopped at a station. A number of people got off but no one came into their compartment. The train moved off again. The Commander stood up, placed his copy of The Times neatly on the seat beside him and walked off to go to the toilet - or the *heads* as he might have called it, being the nautical term for a loo.

When he came back he found the Colonel sitting in his seat.

"This is my seat." The Commander said.

The Colonel glanced up from his paper. "I am sitting here," he said.

The Commander pursed his lips. "But I was sitting here. I just went to the heads."

The Colonel nodded politely. "I am sitting here now, so it is my seat."

Commander Anthony Oliver OBE politely raised his bowler hat an inch off his head. "As you wish," he said calmly. He leaned over to retrieve his nespaper and sat down opposite the Colonel in the seat the Army man had recently vacated.

The Colonel opened the window. The wind rustled his newspaper but he seemed oblivious to it. A faint, grim, smile of satisfaction swept across his lips.

So, it was that the two men sat, I must tell you, in a not unusual British silence, their two faces buried in their newspapers. Whether they were actually reading anything, I couldn't say.

In a few moments the train stopped again at another station.

"Haywards Heath! Haywards Heath!" The station master yelled.

The Commander leaped to his feet, tucking his paper under his arm. He raised his bowler to the Colonel. "Good day to you," he said coolly.

He made as if to leave the compartment.

At the last moment he turned back, holding up a leather glove. "Excuse me," he said, "I think I must have dropped one of my gloves under your seat."

The Colonel looked behind him on the seat, then got up from the seat. He bent over to look underneath. While he was thus engaged, the Commander slid nimbly into the seat and sat down in it.

The Colonel looked up, dumbfounded. "Excuse me," he said.

"This is my seat."

"Not any longer, answered the Commander, in good humour again. "It is my seat. I am sitting in it."

The Colonel stared at him, becoming redder in the face for every moment he stared. Eventually, he raised his bowler an inch. "As you wish."

He sat down on the seat opposite the Commander which the sailor had recently vacated.

The Commander, seeing the window was open, hauled down on the window strap and snapped it shut. Returning to his newspaper, he casually turned over another page of The Times, folding it neatly in half. Smiling to himself, he settled back comfortably in his seat.

Colonel George Grant. VC. glared at him. Then he picked up his cane and smashed a hole in the window with one sudden blow of the heavy silver knob which was its handle. Pieces of glass blew back in over the Commander who looked up from his newspaper.

"Needed some air in here," said the Colonel. "Present company is making it stuffy!"

The Commander who had been under gunfire in the war and had suffered far worse, calmly brushed specks of glass off his suit."

"In another age, I would call you out for that insult," he said.

The Colonel smiled grimly. "By all means," he said. "But I would skewer you in a moment. I am a champion fencer. I founded the Salisbury Fencing Club when stationed with my tanks on Salisbury Plain."

The Commander nodded. "Well, well! It so happens I founded the fencing club in Bath when I was stationed at the Admiralty there."

The Colonel was impressed but didn't say so. He raised his bowler an inch from his head, saying: "Your choice of weapon then, sir...sabre, foil or epee ? At my club or yours?

The Commander, revealing his first moment of irritation, exploded: "Damn your eyes, sir, we'll fight with walking sticks the moment we get off this damn train."

"As you wish," replied the Colonel.

Well, there was only one more stop to go and that was Brighton where both men were due to get off.

The moment they were off the train they walked outside the station to where the taxis were waiting, but instead of ordering a taxi, they stripped off their coats, flinging them on the ground as they took up a classic fencing stance, one with his silver headed cane, the other with his mahogany walking stick, their bowlers remaining on their heads.

On and on they fought, moving back and forth, attempting to penetrate the defences of the other with their sticks. It was evident they were both at the top of their chosen, particular, sporting discipline.

And who won?

As it happened, neither of them won because the Colonel who was becoming increasing frustrated at being unable to score off the nimble Commander, suddenly slashed his cane upward in a massive sabre-like undercut which snapped his cane into two pieces. The force of the blow sent the Commander's stick flying out of the Navy man's hand. It landed under a Brighton bus which was at that moment pulling into the train station, smashing the highly polished mahogany walking stick to bits.

Both men looked astonished at this turn of events. They gaped at each other furiously.

The Colonel gazed at his dismembered cane. The Commander saw the pieces of his once fine walking stick crunched under the bus. When they looked up they saw quite a crowd had gathered. The puzzlement of the crowd was obvious. The two men looked at each other for a long moment. The Colonel saluted his opponent by lifting his broken cane to his bowler. The Commander gave the Colonel a vague Naval salute. They stared at each other, then burst out laughing. Both men were grinning as they picked up their coats.

"I think a quick noggin at the Crown and Anchor is in order," said the Army man.

"No disagreement there," replied the sailor. " The sun is well over the yard arm!"

They went off arm in arm, the Colonel holding on to his truncated cane, the bit with the silver knob on it. The Commander left his shattered walking stick under the bus.

So that is how the Colonel and the Commander became the best of chums, and why they fight a commemorative duel every year to remind themselves of how they met - and, of course, to keep up their fencing skills, albeit with walking sticks!

Also, of course, it is happens to be the perfect excuse to avoid the monotony of old age, and have a decent nosh-up with friends at the Crown and Anchor.

8

THE INTELLIGENT DOG

This is a true story and I will tell it just as it happened. My mother was eighty two at the time and I have to tell you her orchard was getting away from her. What I mean by this, is that it was getting so overgrown by bracken and kikuyu grass, it was becoming a real problem. However hard, I, or my brother, or Nadine, her weekly gardener, tried to keep it down by pulling out the stuff by hand or slashing it with our small tractor, her fruit trees were still being choked by the pervasive African grass, not native to Australia, first planted by early farmers for their dairy cows, which now grew so fast and vigorously in our area. It was becoming quite unmanageable.

"I don't want to use herbicide," she said. "I really

don't. I hate to think what it will do to all the birds and bees and butterflies, in the spring."

She then had a bright idea.

"I know," she said. "I'll get a sheep. It will keep down the grass. There will be plenty of grass in the orchard for a sheep, or even two sheep."

She phoned up her niece, my cousin Viv, who was married to a farmer some miles west of the edge of the town where we lived..

"Certainly, you can have a couple of sheep," he said kindly. "I will bring them round for your birthday."

Sure enough, and good as his word, Ian brought round a couple of leggy looking sheep in his pick-up. They were white Suffolks, a taller breed than Merinos with longer legs. Viv had tied beautiful pink bows tied around their necks to make them look like birthday presents.

"Happy Birthday, Audrey," Ian said cheerfully, giving her a kiss. "Here is your birthday present! Two lovely grass munching lawn mowers for you! They'll do the job for you, no probs!"

He ran the pick-up alongside the orchard fence.

I, who was there at the time and being helpful, went to open the gate.

"Oh no," cried Ian. "No need for the gate. I will chuck them over the fence".

Not knowing much about sheep other than that they were woolly creatures and made a *'baa-ing'* noise, I asked Ian if they were liable to escape or go through fences?

"No," he said. "Only if they are frightened or get in a panic. Then they'll go through a fence, all right. Go through any fence." He seized the first sheep bodily in his arms. It struggled desperately and I have never seen an animal so frightened. Its eyes were starting out of its head in wild terror . He hurled it like a sack of potatoes over the fence into the jungle of bracken, followed shortly afterwards by the second equally terrified lawn mower.

Both sheep landed with a thump and charged off blindly through the thick undergrowth. I couldn't see them, and I am quite sure they couldn't see where they were going, either - anything to get away from the madman who had picked them up and hurled them into this strange place of tangled, five foot high, grass and bracken.

Well, to cut a long story short, they both charged off through the bracken going like steam trains. They hit the fence the other side. I couldn't see a thing but I heard it clanging as they went through it like a dose of salts. And, then I did see them - which was the last time I ever did set eyes on them - as they appeared on the slope beyond the orchard, going on their long legs as if a marauding lion was after them, heading down the hill towards the swamp at the bottom of our property.

"Hey! Look at that!" Exclaimed Ian. "They have escaped. Your fences can't have been up to much."

"I checked them," I replied. "Before you came. The fences were fine. You said if they were frightened they would go through any fence. And they were frightened all right!"

"They shouldn't have been frightened."

There was no point in arguing the matter. I wondered if we would ever get them back.

"Get on to the Shire Ranger," Ian advised. "He'll be able to get them back for you."

And so we did - or at least my mother did.

Audrey phoned the Shire and asked to speak to the Ranger. She explained our problem.

"No problem," the Ranger said. "Just run after them and catch them!"

"What do you mean? These sheep run faster than I do," said my mother. "Even if I was forty years younger

Mark Kumara

I wouldn't be able to catch them. I am eighty two, you know! You try catching them!"

The Ranger hummed and haah-ed and eventually said: "No problem! I'll bring round a sheep dog. Don't you worry, we'll get them back for you."

She put the phone down, turning to me, "I don't think this Ranger knows any more about sheep than you or I do! But he is coming round tomorrow with a sheep dog."

Next day turned out to be one of those rare days we occasionally get when the temperature goes above the old hundred degrees. It was so hot you could hear the gum in the gum trees snapping in the midday heat. It was like breathing air in a furnace.

Nonetheless, the Ranger turned up with his dog in the back of his pick-up. He *had* to come in the middle of the day, of course. And off we all went, all four of us, me, my mum with her walking stick, the Ranger and his dog, down the hill towards the water.

Perhaps I haven't explained, we live on the edge of a big lake - an inlet, really, which goes down to the sea a few miles away.

Now, both Ranger and dog were on the plump side. Fat, I ought to say! Both were also getting on in years. The Ranger was perspiring freely, his stomach hanging over his belt like a lump of suet pudding. His dog looked in no better shape. It was some sort of blue heeler kelpie-cross with nice eyes. Intelligent looking. It waddled along gamely in the heat. Yes, it definitely waddled!

I glanced across at my mother. She glanced at me. I knew what she was thinking. It didn't look much of a dog to me, either! Not the sort to go chasing about the countryside.

Well, maybe in a past life-time!

But we strode slowly down the hill in the sweltering heat.

81

The Ranger must have caught our mood because he said: "He's a sheep dog."

I saw my mother give a twitch of her lips. She knew dogs. She'd been with dogs all her life. As a girl she was always the one who had trained the family dog. Every morning her own dog, Bonny, fetched the newspaper at the bottom of her drive. At the moment, Bonny was shut up in the house so he wouldn't interfere with the Ranger's dog's important mission.

I asked: "Are you sure he's man enough for the job?" The more I studied the dog the less sure I was. It was definitely labouring in the heat. But who was I, to question an expert...I, who knew nothing of sheep? However, being my mother's son I did know something about dogs. And, to me, this dog looked uncommonly like a dog who had not the slightest interest in sheep.

"Don't you worry," said the Ranger confidently. "He'll sniff them out and round them up in a jiffy!"

It was then that I caught my mother's eye again and I could see she was having the utmost difficulty, as was I, in containing her laughter. The impossibility of it - the whole unreality of the situation - flashed between us. It was definitely contagious. Here was the Ranger being so serious about his wonderful dog and here were we in silent stitches in the frazzling heat, trying like anything to hold it in. Every step I took I thought I would explode with embarrassing guffaws. There was no way, we both saw, in a thousand years that this dog was going to chase any sheep - let alone round them up and herd them nicely through the gate into the orchard.

So, what happened?

Well, on reaching the lower part of our block the Ranger began snapping his fingers at the dog, shouting in a voice becoming ever more husky. "Go boy! Go get'em!" But it had not the slightest effect. Sheep was the very last thing on this dog's mind - even if it understood what was required of it, of which I am not at all sure.

At any rate, it paid not the slightest attention to the Ranger.

Head down, tongue lolling, it plodded- waddled I should say - ever closer to the water. Suddenly, there it was. It saw the water stretching out before it like an oasis of cool relief. It didn't hesitate for a second, it waddled into the water, sank gratefully down into it, and there it stayed.

Oh my! What an intensity of relief there was in its doggy body as it sank up to its neck in the lake. It had this truly beatific look of blissful contentment on its face when it finally turned round to look at us. "Are you coming in, too?" It seemed to be asking.

Nothing, absolutely nothing, could persuade that dog to leave the water.

The Ranger, becoming more frustrated by the minute, cursed and swore at the dog. First he called it a good dog, then he called it a bad dog, then he went in after the dog but got his boots stuck in the mud, so had to come back, almost falling over in the process, wiping his brow with a grimy handkerchief and his boots on the grass.. His dog paid him not the slightest bit of notice. It wallowed in the water, grinning happily at us. Nothing bar a bomb was going to move that dog.

Meanwhile, as you can imagine my mother and I were in fits of laughter on the bank. At last, we had let it out! What with the heat and the laughter, it hurt so much, I was bent double and couldn't breathe for a moment. It was actually quite painful. I thought I would die laughing.

I could see we weren't going to get our sheep back today.

Shamefacedly, the Ranger had to admit the same thing. "I don't know what could have got into him.

Mind you," he said, "He isn't my dog. He belongs to a friend who said he was a sheepdog."

So, now he tells us.

Well, that dog didn't come out of the water until we had trudged halfway back up the hill. In the end it reluctantly came out of the water, I suppose, because it didn't want to be left behind.

When we got to the Ranger's pick-up, the dog suddenly became a different dog. You wouldn't have thought it was the same dog. As soon as it saw its ride home, it pricked up its ears, wagged its tail and leaped nimbly into the back of the pick-up, looking as happy as Larry and more alert than any respectable sheep dog, on such a hot day, has ever looked or ever should look. Its eyes were bright. Standing in the back of the ute it wagged its tail happily. It looked ready for anything.

Ready to go home, in fact.

The Ranger, somewhat subdued, drove off, mentioning first to my mother that she might have lost her sheep for ever. What a help that was!

The fact was, we never did see the sheep again. But we did hear rumours that a couple of long legged wild sheep had been seen by bush walkers in the hills nearby. What especially intrigued the walkers, who told their tale to all and sundry at the local pub, was a curious thing: the sheep appeared to be wearing pink bow ties.

Well, you can imagine how that went down, can't you!

Pink elephants, maybe, if you've had a few too many. But, pink sheep?

My mother's last comment on the matter, as we watched the Ranger drive away, was:

"*That*, in my opinion, was a most intelligent dog!"

I had to agree.

9

AMANDA'S STORY

My name is Amanda. I am ten years old and I love my horse who is called Sugar. I don't love my step-mother - well, she's actually my *de facto* step-mother - who is cruel to me, except when anyone comes to the house, and then she pretends to be so loving. It is nauseous! Really nauseous!

My father is away a lot of the time. He is a diplomat, on relief duty, somewhere in southern Russia at the moment, so I have to stay at home with my nauseous step-mother - and my even more nauseous step-sisters.

My step-sister are called Georgina and Adriana. They are both gross. And I think they are actually frightened of my horse who is so gentle and sweet. Of course, their nauseous mother dotes on them. Nothing is too good for them.

Nothing is what I get!

When she writes to my father she tells him how sweet

I am. Tells him how happy I am. I know this because Georgina told me so. What a load of rubbish!

I write to Dad every week but I hardly ever get a reply. I suspect she reads and trashes my letters to him, so I must try to find a way to get to the mail box without her which is not so easy when you live next to a game park in Kenya, miles from anywhere.

And that is another thing, I love being here, in Africa, because I can go riding for miles in the bush with Sugar amongst all the animals which is so cool. You can get so closer to the zebra and buck and giraffe etc on a horse, much closer than you can on foot, but my nauseous step-mother hates being in Kenya. She would like to be back home in her pretty little suburban English garden - or better still, she would like to live in a grand manor house, which Dad has to pay for!

She can't wait to get married to Dad so she can do that!

My father is in the British diplomatic service, you see, and we came out to Nairobi which is the capital of Kenya a year ago, but just recently there was an emergency and he had to go to one of those new countries in Russia to fill in for someone. So, at present we are in a bit of a limbo, we can't join him in Armenia and we can't go home to England because his job is still really here in Kenya.

But, I don't mind. I love it here. I love riding with Sugar out in the bush. It is like going on my own private safari. I am never afraid, even when Sugar and I came face to face with a buffalo the other day on a steep cliff. It was a bit scary because buffalos are very powerful animals and can be quite mean, but Sugar was wonderful she just stared at the buff and I just stared at the buff and the buff stared back at both of us, and then with a big snort it turned and charged up the hill. Gosh! I was happy about that!

My step-mother doesn't care what I get up to: in fact, I don't think she would be at all bothered if the buffalo had charged and trampled us to death or we'd fallen over the cliff. No, I don't think she'd mind that, at all.

In fact, Georgina told me the other day that Dad had written to her mother saying he was leaving everything to her and nothing to me. She said he had made out a new will because he was working in such a dangerous country.

I don't believe her.

Adriana is just as bad, grinning at me like a lump of dough, she said she was sure he was going to die over there. They are so gross. I hate them.

You are right, it sounds like the Cinderella story all over again. I guess that sort of thing *did* happen, I mean, to Cinderella. Well, it's happening to me. Except it is not in a fairy tale. It's real!

But, at least I don't have to clean the house for them or do any of that sort of thing because we have a maid that comes in every day to do that, and we also have a gardener. All the same, my step-mother is cruel and Georgina and Adriana are gross.

At least, I have got Sugar.

She is such a lovely horse. I love her to bits. She's a light chestnut pony. She has a long, elongated, white star on her face and two white socks on her front feet. And she is very good at avoiding ant bear holes which is a real trap for horses in Kenya who are kept in stables all the time. They soon fall down them and break their legs, but Sugar who lives out in a paddock next to our house is very wise to ant bear holes. You should see how, even at a gallop, she nimbly swerves around them or jumps over them, and, of course, I hold her on a loose rein so she can do this. I trust her completely.

So, that is my situation. That is all about me. At least, that *was* my situation. It has changed now. Let me tell you why and how. Let me tell you just as it happened. It is the sort of story you would never believe in a thousand years.

I told you how Georgina had told me Dad was leaving everything to my step-mother - and Adriana saying she hoped Dad would die in Armenia. Well, I was very angry about that, so the next day I went on a very long ride with Sugar to get as far away from all of them as I could, . It makes me feel happy to be amongst the animals. They do their own thing. I am doing my own thing. They are not always putting me down like my dough-faced step-sisters.

Well, that day, Sugar and I went a long way up the escarpment of the rift valley. It's very pretty up there. In the evening, around the hot springs that trickle from the valley walls into small steaming pools you can see fire flies dancing. Today, in the heat of the day, the fire flies weren't there, but there were plenty of wild guinea fowl in the flat topped thorn trees, cackling noisily at us as we passed, and heaps of tommies, as we call them. Thompson's gazelles is their proper name. There were also a few impala with their marvellous bounding leaps. As usual, we got very close to them, especially when we slowed down to a walk.

I saw a pair of dik dik bounding away in the sparse yellow grass. Dik dik are tiny little buck, no taller than my step-mother's poodle, like little Bambis with tiny straight horns. So sweet. There were a few zebra about, too, but we didn't get close to them. Something was obviously worrying them. They were a little jumpy.

A few moments later, I nearly fell off Sugar. We were cantering along when a warthog followed by three little baby piglets suddenly exploded out of the thorn bush in front of us, all going like a rockets, right across our track. Sugar stopped dead and I nearly flew off into the thorn bush.. A good thing I didn't. Those long white thorns are like syringe needles! They'd stick you pretty good! I did lose a stirrup. But, good wonderful Sugar just stood still while I got my balance again, so everything was O.K.

Maybe, I didn't tell you that Sugar, before Dad got her for me, had been partly trained as a polo pony. That means she was trained to stop on her hocks, instead of on her front feet - which is marvellous because it means that if she stops all of a sudden it is like sitting back in a comfortable armchair instead of being thrown forward.

Anyway, the warthog took us both by surprise, but no harm done. That is just one of the exciting things that can happen when you go on safari.

We turned back about three in the afternoon and were back on the flat floor of the valley which was strewn with black volcanic rocks but was otherwise fairly easy going when I heard a humming noise coming from above me. I looked up, and there above me was a flying saucer.

Yes, believe me, this is absolutely true. A flying saucer!

It was quite big and just hovering there in the air above us, making this humming noise. No flashing lights or anything like that, just a big grey silver thing, making this gentle humming noise.

I wasn't frightened. Should I have been frightened? I don't know. Anyway, I wasn't, but I was slightly apprehensive that Sugar might be frightened, though at the time she didn't seem to be.

All the same, to be on the safe side I decided to get off her. I stood beside her looking up at it. The saucer seemed to be in no hurry to leave. It was just sitting there, hovering, seeming to observe me.

Then, to my astonishment, it moved forward a little way and landed on some flat ground in front of us, settling down as softly as thistle down on a tennis court.

The humming noise continued as a door opened and a ramp settled down.

What on earth is happening, I wondered. Am I to be abducted never to be seen again? My step-mother would be pleased!

However, that was not what happened.

Suddenly a voice spoke up. It came from the flying saucer - the space ship - as I now supposed it was.

"You father needs you," the voice said. It was a feminine voice. Very precise. It sounded like my English teacher at home who I thought was really cool. "We will take you to him. Bring your horse. Your father needs your help."

I was so amazed by this, you can't imagine. Or, perhaps you can! Dad needing my help? With my horse? What was this? What was going on here?

Anyway, I didn't think twice. If Dad needed my help, that was that!

Sugar didn't seem the least afraid as I led her up the ramp into the saucer, and down a passage where there was, believe it or not, a hay stall! Next to it was a plastic box brimming with water! She tucked into the hay as if it was the most normal thing in the world, as this was part of her everyday routine.

Wonderful brilliant Sugar!

As I was standing there wondering what on earth was going on, I heard the humming noise alter in pitch slightly. I looked out of a port hole and saw that we were travelling at what must have been a great speed. The ground was absolutely whizzing by. It was not like being in an aeroplane where the ground seems to move by so slowly. This was fast, and I mean *fast*!

I wondered then whether Dad was mixed up in some sort of government secret thing and this saucer was a kind of secret aeroplane. But that thought was soon gone when I met the owner of the voice I'd heard. A panel opposite the hay stall slid open and an alien being walked through it, smiling. She was *so* small, about my height, wearing a silver suit and had big black slanted eyes. In fact, she was just like an alien I had seen in some TV shows. The first thing she said was:

"Thank you for trusting us and not being afraid."

"Who are you?" I said. Maybe it was a silly thing to say, but it just came out. My mind had gone blank.

"Oh, we are human, like you are, but we've been around a bit longer that's all."

"What's happened to Dad?" I asked, my mind beginning to function again.

"We'll be there in a minute. You will see for yourself. Your father is perfectly all right but he needs your help."

I looked out of the port hole. I saw that we were landing. I hadn't heard a thing but the hum of the machine had altered in pitch again. We seemed to be in very rugged country, just below the snow line in a very mountainous region. I wondered where it could be.

"We're in Turkey," she said, and when I turned round again she was handing me a drink in a glass. "A drink," she said. "You must be thirsty after your long ride."

I was, and I took it gratefully. It tasted like guava juice.

"You have heard of the mountain where Noah came to rest in his ark. This is it." She said. "Your father has come to rest here, too." She then handed me some packages. "Food," she explained. "Self-heating. Two days worth." Then she handed me an even bigger package which I saw was a backpack. "In here there is a tent. And some warm clothes, gloves etc. No, they are not alien made," She laughed. "They come from Harrods."

He laugh sounded as if she had the hiccups. Her eyes were moist.

I gave her back the empty glass and slipped on the backpack.

"Is the ark still there?" I asked. I wondered if we were going to see it?

"Long gone. Nothing left of it.

Your horse is very gentle," she said handing me Sugar's rein. "What is her name?"

"Sugar," I said.

She looked a little wistful. "I wish I could ride her like you do."

"Come and visit us, and you can," I said.

She looked at me quite seriously. "I don't know if I will be able to do that but that is very kind."

"Is Dad here, outside?" I asked.

"Close by, over that rise." She pointed. "He can't see us. But you will find him easily. Now, listen carefully. There is a track leading down from where he is. Go south down that track, keep on the track, don't deviate from the track and in two days you will come to a village. You will be safe in the village. From there you can phone your government who will send someone for you."

She put her hand on Sugar's neck and ran her hand down to her ears. And then she did a strange thing; she whispered something into Sugar's ear and then actually bent and kissed her on the nose.

"Goodbye, Sugar," she said. "Look after my new friend." Then she looked lovingly at me. "Goodbye, Amanda, perhaps we will meet again one day."

"Goodbye," I said, "And thank you for your help." I was so excited at the prospect of seeing my father, I wanted to be out of there."

"Always glad to be of help." she said, and that was the last I saw of her, for Sugar and I were now moving down the ramp on some kind of moving conveyor belt, and then, suddenly there we were out in the cold mountain air, surrounded by rocks and patches of snow.

The flying saucer, humming loudly, elevated itself and moved off so fast I could barely follow it. Then it was gone, leaving Sugar and me alone in a strange rocky wilderness.

It was a pretty dismal place all right. Leading Sugar by her rein I picked our way through the lichen covered rocks to the rise which the lady in the flying saucer had pointed out to me, and when we got to the top, there, on the other side, sitting against the remains of a wicker basket, a large coloured balloon strewn behind him over the rocks, was Dad.

He seemed to be dozing, but as we clattered down to him, small stones dribbling away under Sugar's feet, he opened his eyes and saw us.

Never in all my life have I seen such astonishment in anyone's face. He obviously thought we were a ghost or must be hallucinating.

"Good gracious me, Amanda!" He exclaimed. "Is it you? Are you real?"

I rushed into his arms. "I am as real as you are," I shouted joyfully. "I am so glad to see you."

"So am I, so am I, "he kept repeating. "Where on earth did you come from? How did you get here? How did you know where I was?"

"I will answer all your questions," I said. "But first, we have to get going. We have to walk south down this track and in two days we will come to a village where we will be safe and you can phone the embassy."

"How do you know all this ?" he said. "It is all unbelievable. I thought I was going to die here. I got caught in a storm. It whirled me up and really shook me out. I drifted along for ages, completely blacked-out, freezing with cold, not knowing where I was or where I was going and then came down here, on this mountain. My radio was smashed in the crash. I haven't a clue where we are."

"We are in Turkey," I told him. "On Mount Ararat."

He was relieved to hear this. "Well, that's safer than

Russia." Then gave a faint smile. "Noah and I have something in common."

"There's nothing left of his ark," I said.

He shook his head, muttering, "How do you know all this?"

We quickly got going. Sometimes I rode Sugar, and Dad walked beside me. Sometimes Dad rode Sugar and I walked, and some of the time we both walked and gave Sugar a rest.

That night we put up the tent the woman had given me - it was dome shaped - and had hot baked beans and tinned sausages for tea. They were delicious and the tent was cosy. It was so good to be with Dad.

As we walked, I told Dad what had happened. He found it hard to believe. But, on the other hand, what other explanation could there possibly be? That fact, and that fact alone, really stumped him. He was a practical British diplomat whose hobby was ballooning. "I don't believe in flying saucers," he muttered. "Or divine intervention!" He looked at me quite hard, but when he looked again he was smiling. "I don't know," he said. "I really don't know. I guess I will have to believe you!"

I was on safer ground talking about home.

I asked him at one point why had hadn't replied to any of my letters?

"I didn't receive any," he said.

I told him that I had written once a week. I also told him what Georgina had told me about him changing his will leaving everything to my step-mother and what Adriana had said to me about expecting him to die in this place and hoping he would.

He went very silent about that and I could see he was quite disturbed and angry.

"I never got your letters," he said bitterly. "But I got a lot from your step-mother telling me how happy you were, and all the good things she was doing for you."

"All untrue," I said. All totally untrue."

Well, he thought about that for a while. He could see the way the wind had been blowing all right. I could see his jaw tighten as he digested what I had told him.

"There will be some changes when we get back," he said.

And that is all he did say about the matter because just then we topped another rise and there before us, nestling in a valley, was a cluster of houses with telegraph posts marching beyond it into the distance.

We had reached the village. We had reached safety.

Dad immediately phoned the embassy. They said they would send a helicopter for us. I said it had to be a big helicopter, big enough to take Sugar. They weren't happy about that but Dad put his foot down and eventually they agreed to ask for help from the Turkish military who kindly agreed to send a big helicopter suitable for a horse.

So, that is my story. I told you it would be difficult to believe, didn't I?

The end of the story is equally good. Father had a terrific row with my step-mother when we got home. He told her that she was cruel and mean and a liar, and that their marriage was off, and he never wanted to see her again. She and her two horrible daughters went back to England. I never saw them again, either. Thank goodness!

Dad got his old job back in Nairobi and we went back to the same house next to the game park. I really can't be happier.

And Sugar is still very well, too.

When I am riding with her out in the bush, just Sugar and me, and the impala and tommies, and zebra, and the leggy giraffe loping along as if on stilts, and we emerge from beneath the shade of the yellow flat-topped thorn trees onto the flat grassy area alongside Lake Naivasha where the flamingos have settled like a pink cloud, and, when I see the vultures lazily riding the thermals in the hazy distance, I can't help looking up at the sky, now and then, and wondering…just wondering…

10

NANNY MARGARET

My name is Leila. I, absolutely, completely and totally, do not believe that death is the end of everything. I can prove it to you.

At the end of my story you might come to the same conclusion I have: that our being here on earth is just a journey, and the reason we are here is to learn something.

My father has learnt something, all right. He has learnt not to be right all the time.

I think he has also learnt that perhaps science and

logic - his brand of logic, anyway - isn't the answer to everything.

Dad is a scientist. He thinks he knows everything about everything. No one can tell him anything without him making some comment about it, either trying to show that they are wrong - or that he knows better than they do. It is so boring and makes him look so silly. But, all the same, I do love him to bits. He is sometimes very funny and makes us all laugh and reads me wonderful stories at bedtime, some of which he makes up himself. If he gets stuck, I help him out. We have made up some very good stories like this. One day I might write them down.

I have an elder sister called Mary and two older brothers, Ray and Alwyn. As we are such a big family, we have a nanny. Her name is Bertha. She is lovely and great fun. She is Welsh, by the way, and sings beautifully. One day I would like to be able to play the piano and sing like her. Who knows, maybe I will.

Before Bertha, we had Nanny Margaret who very sadly died. This story is really about Nanny Margaret. It was a shock when she died because, you see, I had known Nanny Margaret all my life. We all loved her to bits and so did Mummy. Like Mummy, Nanny Margaret hardly ever raised her voice but when she did we all jumped to attention!

I know Mummy was fond of Margaret because she always remembered her birthday and put a Christmas present for her under the tree, which she wrote down on the card as coming from Father Christmas.

We all knew who it was really from, of course!

Nanny Margaret was very good at teaching us things like painting and sewing, making cloth dolls - and even chess. She was quite good at chess. She even beat Daddy sometimes who was meant to be very good at chess. She particularly loved playing dress-up and making up little plays in which all five of us would take part. It was a lot of fun. Mummy and Daddy would sit back and laugh their heads off. Margaret would always take us to the circus when it came to Bournemouth. One year she went with us to the pantomime at Christmas when Daddy was away, and I remember seeing tears in her eyes when it was over. I think her secret dream was to be an actress. But, of course, that never happened. She was our nanny.

Now, about my story. This is what happened:

It was the summer holidays.

When my elder sister and my brothers were back from boarding school we always, every year, went to Bude in Cornwall for two weeks. We stayed with Mummy's sister who had a big house there right on the coast. It was always a lot of fun. Not least, because without nanny - nanny never went to Cornwall with us - we saw lots of Mummy and Daddy who took us to the beach, went kite flying with us on the old hill forts that were always very windy places, and had picnics in all sorts of other special places like old ruined castles and smugglers' coves where the tin miners carved deep tunnels to hide their contraband in, and, of course, we always went with Aunty Jessica to Land's End and her favourite tea shop.

It was the time of year when Nanny Margaret took her two weeks holiday. This year, she told us, she was going to France. She had always wanted to go to Paris, and this was the year she was finally going to go. It was a great adventure for her. She said she wanted to sit in a cafe on the Champs Elysee and have croissants and red wine, and climb the Eiffel Tower. She might also go to a few shows.

Well, I was so excited about going on the train the next day to Cornwall, I found it hard to sleep that night. We had spent the day packing. I had to do most of my own packing because nanny had gone off the previous day to catch the ferry to Dieppe. My small suitcase was sitting in my room by the dressing table and I kept looking at it and wondering if I had remembered to take everything. The only things I had to remember to put in the morning were my washing things, and Peter - Peter, if I haven't told you already, is my teddy. I didn't have room for my dolls. Only Peter was coming to Cornwall with me .

I kept dropping off to sleep. Then waking up. Peter was next to me as he always is. I would give him a cuddle and then go off to sleep again.

Suddenly, in the middle of the night, Nanny Margaret came in to see me. I woke up and there she was, just standing there. That is not as odd as it might seem because she would often visit us in the night if she thought we weren't sleeping or were having some difficulty like having a coughing fit - or just to check on us. I didn't really think anything of it, even when I remembered that nanny had said she was going to France and had gone off the day before. I naturally assumed she had come back for some reason or other.

Nanny looked at me with that sweet smile of hers, and, I remember this very well, she said in her soft voice: "Say goodbye to Peter for me." She reached out a hand to stroke my hair as she often did, but then withdrew it again as if having second thoughts, and then she vanished.

I mean, she actually seemed to sort of fade out through the wall. It was so strange. I didn't hear the door open or anything like that. She simply disappeared.

However, I didn't think much of it at the time. I was soon asleep and for the rest of the night I slept right through, waking early, as excited as ever at the thought of going down to Cornwall on the train.

I often go to see Mummy and Daddy in the mornings, and get into bed with them, and have a cuddle, but this morning I heard them arguing.

My father was saying: "I don't believe in things like that. It must be your imagination."

My mother had raised her voice a bit, which she rarely did and I heard her say. "You can say what you like, but I *did* see nanny last night."

On that note, I bounced into their room, saying "I saw her, too!"

"Who did you see, darling?" Asked Mummy.

"I saw nanny. She must be back. She said goodbye to Peter!"

My father opened his mouth and shut it again.

My mother put her hand over his. "Darling, what time did you see nanny?"

"I don't know what time it was. It was in the middle of the night. But she's come back. I saw her, then she vanished."

"How do you mean...she vanished?" My father asked gruffly.

"I don't know," I said. "She was there one moment, then she disappeared. She didn't open the door, she sort of walked through the wall. Like magic!" I said boldly. I was always a girl who was fond of mysteries.

My father gave a snort of laughter.

"Yeah! Yeah! Very funny! I know. You two have concocted this up between you! I can see we are going to have a great holiday this year - with ghost stories on the menu. Run along now, Leila, we have to get up and get ready for the train."

My mother didn't say a word, but as I was walking away, I heard her say: "We haven't concocted anything. This is not a joke we've made up. Margaret came in, said goodbye to me, then walked through the door."

I thought about this. Something peculiar was going on, so I went to Margaret's room to find her. She wasn't there. I asked cook where she was. Cook said she had gone to France. It was all most peculiar, but then we were off to Cornwall and everything went out of my mind except to get ready with my brothers and sister for the train.

Some weeks later, I asked my mother about it. She was happy to tell me. She told me that nanny had appeared to her by her bed in the middle of the night.

But, she knew nanny was in France. She said with astonishment, "Margaret, what are you doing here?"

Apparently, nanny said nothing, just looked at her, smiled sweetly and mouthed the words *goodbye*. She then turned and glided back through the door. Nanny didn't open the door. *She went through the closed door.*

I told Mummy that when nanny came to see me she had actually spoken out loud. I had clearly heard her voice.

"What did she say?" she asked.

"Say goodbye to Peter for me."

My mother smiled.

At the time, of course, I knew nothing of this. I just assumed nanny must have forgotten something she wanted to take to France with her. She'd come back to collect it and then gone off again. If the weather was rough the ferry from Newhaven to Dieppe might also be cancelled for a day or two. What else was I to think?

Well, we all bundled into the taxi to take us to the train station, Daddy being as jumpy as usual. He could never stand the thought of being late.

"Hurry up! Hurry up!" He kept shouting, as he usually did whenever we had to go anywhere.

As usual, of course we got to the station far too early and had to wait around for ages for the train. But that was my father for you! Always in a hurry, then waiting around. Stupid really!

Anyway, shortly before the train arrived, Mummy

suddenly announced we weren't going on the train, after all.

"Why on earth not?" My father cried out, looking harassed and perplexed.

"Margaret has told me not go on this train," she said.

"What do you mean?"

"I have just heard her voice, telling me not to go on this train," my mother said calmly.

Then my father really blew up. He was so angry. He really hit the roof. There we were, all six of us, having spent days getting ready, with all our luggage strewn around on the platform and here was Mummy saying we weren't going on the train because Margaret had told her not to - except Margaret was in France and nowhere to be seen.

I don't suppose you could blame him really.

"You stupid woman!" He raged. "Hearing voices in your head! Why do you do this?" He banged his walking stick on the paved surface of the platform as if he was beating a stubborn horse. "Of course, we are taking the train. I won't hear another word of this foolishness!"

But, my mother was made of sterner stuff.

"All right," she said. "If you insist, you take this train. But, the children and I will catch the next one."

My father raged some more, cursing and swearing at women in general, smashing his cane over and over again against some railings. I have never seen him so angry in public. My sister Mary went to hide behind a pillar.

Eventually, he calmed down. It was just as the train was pulling in - the train to Cornwall which we were not going to take, after all.

"Oh, all right! All right! We'll take the next one. I'm not going on my own, leaving you behind. Next, you'll be hearing voices telling you not to go at all, and I'll be at your sister's house in Cornwall on my own, looking like a silly fool!"

So, that was decided. We would take the next train - which happened to be in another two hours.

What did we do?

Leaving the luggage at the station to be looked after by a porter, we took a taxi home again. After all, our home was only five minutes away by car.

Mother asked cook, who was surprised to see us back so soon, to rustle up some sandwiches and coffee while she rang her sister to tell her we'd be arriving on a later train.

Just as we were finishing our second breakfast, as it were, the door bell rang. It was a telegram boy with a telegram for father. Father opened it with a knife while sipping his coffee. When he'd read it he put it face down on the table and slid it over to Mummy. He looked pale.

Mummy read the telegram and bent over the table with her face in her hands.

"What's wrong?" We cried out. We knew something bad had happened.

"Is it nanny?" I blurted out without thinking.

"Yes. I'm afraid it's about nanny," Mummy said, looking up. "Nanny has died in France. She has been killed in a car crash."

We were all shocked, but didn't have much time to dwell on it. The taxi had returned and off we all went to the station again, to collect our luggage and get on the train to Cornwall.

I am happy to tell you that this time there were no voices telling my mother not to go on the train. We all boarded the train which duly set off for Cornwall.

However, it did seem to be taking longer than usual, and father eventually worked out that we were taking a different route from that which we usually took. He asked a ticket inspector who came into our carriage whether we were going by a different way?

"Yes, it's true. We are having to take another line."

"Why would that be?" Enquired my father.

"Well," the ticket inspector said. "Bad news, I'm afraid. The fact is, the previous train crashed down the line at St Ives. The line is going to be blocked for some time. Also, I am sorry to say there have been lives lost."

We were all shocked to hear this. Today seemed to be a day of shocks, one after the other.

My father went very quiet. He went quite white and didn't say anything much for the remainder of the trip but spent the time gazing out of the window. I suppose it was a hard thing for him to take.

Which is how I know - I know absolutely, completely and totally - that there is life after death.

Nanny Margaret was looking after us even after she had passed over to the other side.

11

THE FLY IN THE SANDWICH

Leila was seven years old when her mother said she should learn to play the piano.

Her two older brothers and sister had all began at seven, her mother said, so it was time for her to start, too.

Once a week the piano teacher arrived at their house in Bournemouth, spending most of the morning and some of the afternoon sitting at the piano with her brothers and sister in the drawing room, where the piano was. She made them play interminable scales, Bach's fugues and Mozart sonatas, then gave them endless homework to practice. Now, it was her turn.

But Leila didn't like the piano teacher. She couldn't put her finger on it, she just didn't like her. To begin with she *smelt*. She smelt of a combination of mothballs and greasy bacon, mingled with cheap perfume.

Not only that, she had hairs on her chin and a very prominent mole on her right cheek which had black whiskers sticking out of it which, when you were sitting next to her for a whole hour, was very off-putting.

It probably wasn't her fault that she had piggy eyes and wore spectacles with thick lenses and heavy brown frames, but it all added up to the fact that Leila found Mrs Farwell - for that was the name the music teacher went by - to be an altogether unattractive person.

She couldn't help it. She just didn't like her, and that was that!.

Leila wouldn't have minded learning the piano if it had been Bertha teaching them. Bertha was their nanny. She was a young Welsh woman. She hadn't been with them for very long but already the children adored her. With Bertha they had wonderful sing songs. Their mother even sang along with them in the drawing room some evenings while their father sat in his favourite chair smoking his pipe.

But, her mother wouldn't hear of it. "Nanny has got enough to do without having to teach you music," she said. "Also, she is not a trained music teacher. She just knows how to plays these songs. You have to learn to read music and have a proper musical background."

But, Leila didn't want a proper musical background, whatever that was. Bach's fugues and Mozart's sonatas didn't do much for her. She wanted to play Bertha's kind of songs.

"When I grow up I want to write happy songs you can sing to." She said.

You couldn't help liking Bertha, she was such a happy person. She was always such fun to be with. Whether you were tip-toeing along in the quiet beech woods or on top of a hill with a gale blowing, there always seemed to be a song to sing.

Mrs Farwell, on the other hand, seemed to be such a dried up fossil of a person having no interests other than teaching music which she did just for the money, anyway. Another thing, she hated the outdoors, especially anything to do with animals. Insects she hated with a passion.

Only last week, Mrs Farwell had spotted a spider on the ceiling above the piano. She had yelled and screamed and run out of the room, making a terrible fuss, refusing to go back until the spider had been removed.

This was the sort of woman she was. She was also a terrible gossip.

Bertha jokingly called her the 'Have you heard lady' because she was always saying *have you heard* this, or *have you heard* that...about things happening in the town. *"Have you heard the butcher's wife, was caught shop-lifting,* or *have you heard they are going to make the old cemetery into a golf course."*

That sort of thing.

Well, anyway, Leila did begin her music lessons with Mrs Farwell, but she wasn't doing very well. She was clumsy over her scales and usually forgot to practice. Mrs Farwell told her mother she didn't think Leila was cut out to learn the piano.

"Rubbish!" Said her mother. "Leila loves music. She adores to sing and has a lovely voice. She listens to her CD player all day long. You must persevere with her."

"Yes, Ma'am," said Mrs Farwell. "I'll do my best."

Leila's mother was the sweetest mother anyone could ever wish for. She hardly ever raised her voice, and never ever raised her hand in anger against the children, but there was steel in her all the same; there *were* a few things she was firm about, and learning music was one of them. When Leila's mother was a teenager, a talent scout had seen her dance. He said she should to go to London to train at a music academy, but her mother - Leila's grandmother - had put her foot down. No daughter of hers was going on the stage! She had said. It wasn't proper.

Leila's mother had not forgotten it. And, now, times had changed. She was determined her own daughter would have every chance of learning music if she wanted to - and go on stage, as well.

Well, now, it so happens that one of Leila's brothers, who was a great tree climber, had found a squirrel's nest in a beech tree. There were three baby squirrels in the nest. Putting one of the babies under his jumper, he brought it back to the house as a pet - at least, he hoped it would make a good pet.

And, so it proved to be. It was the sweetest pet you could possibly imagine. After a few weeks, it was so at home in the house, it provided ongoing entertainment for everyone. All day long, it ran up and down the curtains, leaping from picture to curtain rail and back again, leaping, jumping, flying through the air, here and everywhere. All day long it played. It was never still except when, thoroughly exhausted by its play, it would curl up in a comfy warm place somewhere, curl its bushy red tail around its soft furry body, and go to sleep.

Leila's mother didn't mind this new playful guest in the house one little bit. All, including her father, were soon captivated by the adorable creature. It was everyone's favourite. The dogs soon got used to it - it was far too quick for them to catch - and the cats, totally bewildered at first by its mischievous and indefatigable energy, also soon accepted it as a new, if rather strange, member of the household.

In the nursery, the little red squirrel would sit on Bertha's shoulder when she was reading the children a story. At other times it would curl up on her lap. It seemed to like Bertha more than anyone.

The only person who had no time for the squirrel was Mrs Farwell.

"I can't have that thing bounding about in the drawing room while I am teaching," she announced. "It is terrible the way it gets on to the piano and chatters at me!"

Which it did. The squirrel leaped from the curtain rail onto the piano as soon as it saw the music teacher sitting there.

Then it made another leap on to the music stand, chattering furiously at Mrs Farwell as if she was some enemy to be scared away. It obviously didn't like the music teacher - or her music - any more than Leila did.

The last straw came when the squirrel pulled apart Mrs Farwell's sandwiches one day, leaving pieces of them scattered on her tray and all over the room. After that, when Mrs Farwell came to teach, her brother had to lock the squirrel away in his bedroom.

It so happens, on this particular, fateful, day, after her elder sister's music lesson had finished, her brothers, whose turn it was to have their lesson, couldn't be found. Apparently, they had gone to the dentist.

"They won't be long." The maid said. She brought Mrs Farwell a cup of tea in the drawing room. The music teacher settled down to wait for them.

A little later, Leila, creeping past the drawing room, hoping she wouldn't be noticed, saw Mrs Farwell standing by her mother's writing bureau. She was amazed to see the music teacher sorting through her mother's letters, reading them. She saw Mrs Farwell stuff one of the letters into the cloth handbag she carried everywhere with her.

"The nosy gossipy creature!" Leila said to herself. She is she stealing Mum's letters so she has something else to gossip about!"

This proved that Mrs Farwell was not a person to

be trusted. She was definitely not a nice person to have around. Not at all!

Leila made a plan.

And, the plan was this.

You see, at around midday it was Mrs Farwell's habit to take a break. During her break the maid would bring her a plate of sandwiches and a cup of tea.

Off to the kitchen went Leila. Sure enough, she found the maid in the kitchen, preparing the music teacher's sandwiches. She asked if she could take the sandwiches to Mrs Farwell?

"Of course you can," said the maid. "That's very kind."

But, Leila wasn't doing it to be kind, oh dear me no! She had another idea, entirely.

Yes, it had to be a fly!

Where could she find a fly? The bigger the better!

While waiting for the sandwiches to be finished, she saw a big juicy fly (a blue bottle) buzzing against the window in the kitchen. Quickly, she squashed it with the fly squatter which was kept handy for just such occasions. The maid looked up briefly. She nodded approvingly.

She didn't see Leila put the mangled fly in her pocket.

Carrying the tray of sandwiches to the drawing room Leila stopped for a moment in the passage. Resting the tray on a table, she carefully prized apart the top sandwich and slipped the fly neatly between two slices of cold roast beef. Then she took the tray along to the drawing room and gravely handed it to Mrs Farwell.

"Thank you, Leila, that's very nice," said Mrs Farwell who settled down to eat her sandwiches.

Leila sat beside her, watching her intently. The first two sandwiches were quickly eaten. Mrs Farwell, licking her lips, had obviously enjoyed them.

"You don't have to watch me eat," said Mrs Farwell testily. "Run along, girl. I'll ring my little bell when I am ready for you."

Leila stared back at her with her big blue eyes, looking the very picture of innocence. "Oh, but I do," she replied. "I am glad you are enjoying what I put in your sandwich."

"What was that, dear girl? Beef and mustard, I think."

"And a blue bottle," said Leila. "You have just eaten a fat fly I put in your sandwich. I caught it in the kitchen."

What happened next is hard to describe. In short, Mrs Farwell had hysterics. She screamed and yelled, first going white, then purple, and then started to froth at the mouth. Then she started having convulsions.

At that point, Leila's mother, just back from taking her brothers to the dentist, and hearing the commotion, rushed into the room. Behind her, her two brothers stood at the door with their mouths agape at all the fuss.

"What is going on?"

But, Mrs Farwell couldn't speak. She pointed at Leila and screamed and frothed at the mouth, her spittle flying everywhere. Then she fell against the sofa having more convulsions.

"Leila, what is it?" asked her mother again.

"Mummy, she has eaten a fly," explained Leila. "I put it in her sandwich."

"Well, I really don't know," said her mother. "I suppose we had better call the poor woman a taxi." And this they did.

While waiting for the taxi, Mrs Farwell, still moaning, still hysterical, began yelling out the most appalling obscenities. But she was bundled into the taxi, and was never seen again.

After the taxi had left, Leila's mother looked at her

daughter, a little shocked. "Dear, you really shouldn't do that sort of thing, you know."

Which was all she ever said about the matter. That was the sort of mother she was.

Now, I forgot to mention, what with all the drama and the rush to get her into the taxi, the music teacher left her handbag behind. It had to be taken to her in another taxi. But, first, Leila removed her mother's letter from it. She didn't read it. It was private. You didn't read other people's letters.

She handed it to her mother.

"I saw her going through your writing things," Leila said. "I didn't know what else to do. I saw her take it and put it in her bag."

Her mother took the letter, looked at it briefly and a blush spread up her face.

"One of your father's," she said. Telling me how much he loves me." She smiled. "You are a good girl, Leila," she said. "You did well."

"Can I have Bertha teach me the piano?" Asked Leila.

Her mother thought for a moment, her face brightening. "Why not! She might as well. I don't think we'll be seeing Mrs Farwell again."

So that is what happened, which is how Bertha, as well as being a nanny, got to teach Leila the piano. Which is also how, Leila fell into music as if it was a comfortable old slipper just waiting for her.

Leila, today, is one of the finest folk and country musicians in the world, bringing happiness with her beautiful songs to millions of people.

Her mother and father are very proud of her. And so, of course, is Bertha.

And, of course, I mustn't forget to tell you that Leila loves to have squirrels in her garden. Everyday she puts out nuts for them in little baskets hanging from her veranda.

In the summer, when she leaves her windows opens they venture inside.

If you visit her, you will most likely see them scampering up and down her curtains while she is sitting at her piano practicing her songs.

12

THE RUB

One day, Timmy, who was about twelve, was rummaging around in the attic.

His father had told him there might be a fishing rod up there which he could use.

He was excited about this as the rod he had at the moment was only good for fishing off the jetty. It was far too small for casting into the surf where the salmon were. You needed a big rod for salmon. They were big fish and fought like anything.

He hadn't been in the attic very often because it was difficult to get to. You had to pull down a drop-down ladder which was quite stiff and heavy to manage.

Also, his father had told him, he couldn't to go up there unless he had permission first. But, today was different. He had got permission to look for the fishing rod.

"Don't touch anything else," his father had warned.

The attic was full of junk. Anything his parents weren't using and didn't want to throw away they put up in the attic. There were suitcases, some stuffed with old photos. There was an old guitar, a tin trunk, a mirror on a broken stand, a few pictures in ornate frames and another stack of black wooden frames without pictures. There were heaps of books bound with string and cardboard boxes filled with Readers' Digests. Everything was covered with a thin layer of grey dust. It was obvious no one had been up there for a long time.

Switching on his torch, Timmy soon saw the fishing rod which was resting against what looked like an old bathroom stool. It was the type of stool which doubled as a container you could put dirty clothes in. Delightedly, he held the two lengths of the fishing rod in his hands and rubbed off some of the dust, and spiders' webs which were hanging off the end of it. He saw it had a few rings missing but that could be fixed. He looked around the loft, there were plenty of cobwebs up there hanging from the rafters but nothing else he wanted.

On a whim, however, before leaving, he lifted up the lid of the stool and peered inside.

His torch played over some linen which looked like old bed sheets.

Having a feel around to see if there was anything else in there, he found to his surprise there was. There was something hard and round, and heavy wrapped up in a stained yellow pillow case.

Curious to see what it might be, he unwound the pillow case and saw it was a bronze pot. It was obviously old because the bronze was dull and unpolished.

In some places it was tarnished with dark splodges. And it was surprisingly heavy.

Timmy shone his torch upon this strange object. What was it? It looked too wide and squat to be useful as a flower pot. It was the sort of thing you might put on a dressing table to put in spare keys and coins and nail files. Maybe, long ago, in some oriental land it had held nuts or figs, or been a finger bowl?

Whatever it was, all about the top of it, entwined with strange animals which seemed to be prancing around its rim, was a funny looking script. He had never seen anything like it. It could have been from another world.

Looking at it more closely, he saw words had been cut into the lower part of the bowl. They were ingrained with dirt, so he rubbed at them with his sleeve to get a closer look.

These words were definitely in English.

As he rubbed away the dirt, he saw an arrow pointing upwards and the words became clear. **BEWARE! RUB THIS WAY ONLY.**

At that very moment a genii appeared before him. Timmy nearly dropped the pot with shock. The genii was purple in colour and had a long face like a horse. It's eyes gleamed with a greenish light and it said loudly:

"Turn off that torch. It hurts my eyes."

Timmy did so, managing to place the pot on the stool. His heart was thumping like a steam hammer.

"What...wha..." he stammered.

"You have rubbed me up the wrong way!"

"I'm sorry," said Timmy. "I was trying to read what it said."

"A likely story," the genii replied. "I've heard that one before. It won't do you any good. You have one reverse wish."

"A reverse wish? What is that?"

"It means you get a wish, but, the opposite of what you wish for will come true."

"One wish," repeated Timmy. "You mean I have to wish for the opposite of what I really want?"

"Yes," the genii said testily.

"That's unfair," protested Timmy.

"You rubbed me downwards which is the opposite of what you should have rubbed if you wanted a proper wish, so you get an opposite wish. Do you understand? What is your a wish?"

"What I wish for, I get the opposite...is that right?"

"Yes, hurry up. I can't keep floating around here in your attic for ever! It's full of cobwebs, if you haven't noticed!"

Timmy thought about it for a moment. He would have to be careful!

"Do I have to have a wish?"

"Don't try to be a clever! Of course you have to have a wish."

"All right, I'll have a wish." Timmy said. "This is my wish. When I grow up I want to be an ugly, poor, man."

The genii smirked at him. Timmy didn't like the smirk. He was about to say something more when the genii vanished back into the pot, leaving in the air behind him the faintest wisp of purple mist and a lingering smell of stale curry.

Well, the fact is, shortly afterwards Timmy did become fabulously wealthy because an uncle left him a castle in Scotland and millions of dollars to go with it. Not far from the castle was a river which had plenty of salmon in it.

Timmy was, also - everyone thought - the prettiest boy anyone had ever seen.

The extraordinary thing was: instead of growing up, he began to grow *down*. Yes, that's right! He never grew up. He grew down.

He did he not grow up to be a *man*. He grew *down...* and, even more astonishingly, began changing into a *girl*.

But, he did, everyone thought, remain very beautiful.

He stayed looking about ten years old for ever and ever.

Wasn't that amazing!

However, he - or should I say *she* - did become good at fishing!

13

DECENT EXPOSURE

My name is Rosie and the school teacher I like the best is Miss Dippity.She is our maths teacher and I really like her because before she came along I was very bad at maths, and now I am quite good at it. It is still not my favourite subject but Miss D - as we call her - teaches Maths in a really fun way. She takes it slow, so we can understand it and, although Maths can be quite tricky, she says, if you know the tricks - formulae, she calls them - it makes it easy.

Miss D is not only good at the tricks in numbers, and

teaching them to us, she is also good at all sorts of other tricks.

For instance, Robbo, who is in our class and sits at the back near the window, is a real jerk. He is always playing around and pretending to be clever when he is really a dumb dork.

The other day, he was flying paper kites about the class. He thought it was so cool but Miss D caught him and said if he did it again, she would give him a real flying lesson.

Of course, he smirked like he always did.

Then the silly idiot did it again.

Miss D is quick, it's like she has eyes in the back of her head. Anyway, she caught him flying another kite. She didn't say a word. She just pointed her finger at him and he flew out of his desk like a fat balloon and stuck to the ceiling, his back and his bottom sticking to the ceiling like a fly stuck to fly paper.

I couldn't believe it. No one could. It was so weird. You couldn't believe it. But there he was, all right. Stuck to the ceiling like a fat fly with his legs and arms waving about and looking as scared as a six year old's first day at school.

Then it started raining. Though, it wasn't rain. Fatso Robbo was so scared that he wet his pants and his pee was falling down all over his desk. It was gross!

What happened, then?

Well, what happened then was simple. He just floated back down again. Miss D said he better go to the toilet and clean himself up, which he did. He couldn't get out of there fast enough. And, when he came back, he was quiet as a lamb. There was no smirk on his face, I can tell you!

You see what I mean. That was some trick, wasn't it!

Another time, I was being persecuted by Angel who sits next to me, who is anything but an angel. She's really dumb but likes to sit in front with me and pretend she's bright. She is always cribbing off my work. She is a real pain. She is always doing horrible things to me - at least, she used to until Miss D stepped in.

This is what happened.

Angel was nudging me with her elbow as I was trying to write which made my biro slip, making a mess over my work. I told her to stop but she wouldn't. She can be such a dill.

Then, when Miss D was at the back of the class looking at some kid's work, she started nuzzling my neck in a stupid way, saying things like: "Is Mummy's little girl wearing Mummy's expensive perfume, today," and stupid things like that.

I really hate it when she does things like that.

Miss D saw what she was doing and told her to stop being a menace.

Of course, that made Angel worse than ever. She began kicking me under the desks. Miss D saw that, too, and told Angel if she didn't stop tormenting me she'd have something coming her way.

Well, she stopped for a few minutes, but as soon as Miss D's back was turned, she pulled at my hair violently - as if *her* being found out was all my fault!

Well, that did it. I don't know how, but, somehow, Miss D saw. She turned quick as lightening and pointed her finger at Angel. Suddenly all Angel's hair fell off. Yes, it did! I was flabbergasted, but Angel shrieked and sobbed, and then fainted. Angel was particularly fond of her hair. She wore it fluffed and buffed in front, and tied at the back with a ribbon as if she was going on stage or something. She said her mother said she could be a film star. As if pigs could fly!

Well, on that day in class, she was suddenly as bald as a billiard ball and her hair with its pink ribbon was flopped down between us on the desk like an abandoned hair-piece.

I was so shocked I didn't know whether to laugh or anything, but I guess I was glad Miss D was on my side and not hers!

What happened next?

It was weird. Angel came to, grabbed her hair and plonked it back on her bald head, all askew, like she was putting on a wig, then rushed out of the room, holding her hair to her head like someone demented.

She burst into the headmaster's study, screaming blue murder about what Miss D had done to her.

"What's the problem?" The head master said in his usual kindly fashion.

"Mrs Dippity has taken my hair and made it into a wig!" Screamed Angel.

"I see nothing wrong with your hair," the headmaster replied mildly. "Except it looks a bit awry."

"Look!" Cried Angel dramatically - she liked being dramatic - tugging at her hair. "I'll show you!" She gave her hair another hard tug. "Ouch!" She cried again. "It won't come off."

The head master looked at her as if she was ill.

"I think it's better if you go home for the day," he said. "Take the rest of the day off. And get your mother to fix your hair. It looks all over the place."

At tea break, in the common room, the headmaster told Miss D he had sent Angel home.

"She told me some weird story about you taking off her hair and making it into a wig," he said to Miss Dippity. "I've sent her home." He chuckled as he drank his tea. "These girls with their imagination!"

Miss D also smiled. "Thank you, headmaster," she replied, "I'm sure that's a good idea."

And, so it proved. Angel didn't come back to school for two days but, when she did, she really was like an angel, a proper angel, believe me, you have never seen anyone quite so quiet and demure, and subdued, in all your life. She'd also had her hair cut short. There was now a parting at the side where, before, the parting had been in the middle. Strange, wasn't it!

She never bullied me again, not ever. At least, not in Miss D's class.

After that, when anyone in class was told by Miss D to behave they did so very quickly. No one wanted what happened to Robbo and Angel to happen to them.

By the way, I tried mentioning it to Mum and Dad, but they thought it was a huge joke.

"You have such an imagination," chuckled my father. "You should write stories!"

So, I kept quiet about Miss Dippity and, I suppose, for the same reason, did all the other children in our class. I mean, who would believe us?

However, as I say, I did become quite good at Maths.

Miss D had been at our school, teaching our class Maths for about a year when a government inspector of schools came to our school.

As usual, he sat in on school classes in turn to see how well, or badly, we were being taught. In our classroom he was given a spare desk at the side of the room, putting his briefcase beside the desk. He sat there occasionally wiping his spectacles. Every now and then he wrote something down on the clipboard he carried everywhere with him.

Well now, it so happened, the day before Missd D had promised us she would, just for fun, teach us about the tricks that gamblers used at casinos to try to boost their winnings.

"It's all about the odds," she said. "Sometimes you can improve your chances by knowing the odds so you can either keep playing or stop playing at a certain time.

It is all to do with numbers and knowing how they can work for you."

The government inspector began scribbling furiously on his pad. Miss D looked across at him and smiled.

"Wouldn't you agree?" She nodded to the government inspector.

He said gruffly. "It's not my habit to interfere with what's being taught in a class. But, if you really want my opinion. Gambling is not a suitable subject for a Maths class. It is not in any syllabus I am aware of." He scribbled something else down on his pad.

"I try to make Maths fun," Miss D said mildly. "It can be such a dry subject for many children. I try and show them that it can be relevant in everyday life."

"I am not sure that exposure to gambling is a good idea." Replied the schools' inspector primly.

"I am not exposing them to gambling, just to numbers."

The inspector pursed his lips. "It will go down in my report," he said tightly.

"I think not!" Said Miss D in a tone of voice we had all heard before.

"In my opinion, it is still exposure to something not very edifying." Said the inspector. "It will be in my report."

We all held our breath. We had all seen what Miss D could do when she got that glint in her eye!

And, by gosh, she did it! She pointed her finger at the government schools' inspector and his trousers fell down around his ankles. They fell right down to his ankles and stayed there. He tried bending down under the desk to pull them up but they wouldn't come. He tugged and heaved but they wouldn't come up.

He got so red in the face and in such a panic that he upturned the desk. His clipboard and other notes flew all over the floor. His briefcase toppled over.

With his trousers still locked about his ankles, he tried shuffling to the door. Under his blue and white pin-striped shirt you could see he was wearing a rather handsome pair of bright pink underpants with black polka dots all over them. They fairly glowed. There were a few titters from the class, then general laughter broke out. The inspector looked so comical with his trousers down at his feet and his pink bottom with black polka dots, wobbling from side to side as he tugged at the door.

But the door wouldn't open. Most mysteriously, it had seized up. He tugged and heaved, then started cursing and swearing at the door but it still wouldn't open. Then, to add to his final embarrassment, his underpants fell off as well. Down they went to his ankles, to keep his trousers company, and there he was with his naked bottom shining like a big white moon for all of us to see.

It was hilarious. So hilarious. I have never laughed so much in all my life. It was definitely the funniest thing you could ever wish to see.

Just then, however, the door did open. Falling backwards, he clung to it, desperately managing to stay upright, then shuffled - almost falling over again in his haste to get away - out of the classroom.

Unfortunately for him, the headmaster was just coming down the passage to see what all the noise was about.

"What's all this!" The astonished headmaster cried. "Indecent exposure? In front of my children?"

The government inspector, purple in the face, attempted to pull up his underpants. With a struggle, and to his great relief, he did eventually manage to hoist them up But, he couldn't say a word.

"Urrr…!" He spluttered.

"Is this the kind of thing you do? I don't know if you are in the right job?" Said the headmaster.

"My trousers…they fell down and I couldn't get out of the door," the inspector said, finally getting out some words.

"A likely story," Replied the headmaster tartly.

"She did it! Your Maths teacher did it to me."

The headmaster stared at him as if he was a raving lunatic. "An even more likely story."

"No!" Shrieked the government inspector of schools, "It's true. She was exposing the children to things they shouldn't be exposed to."

"Yes, I do see," said the headmaster dryly. "I see exactly the sort of thing they shouldn't be exposed to. "I think it's best if you leave our school straight away."

Well, that was the end of him. That inspector never came back to our school - in fact, I don't know if he ever went back to any school, ever again.

And, what about Miss Dippity?

She announced in class one day, she would be leaving. I was sad. We were all sad. I think even Robbo and Angel were sad about her leaving.

"I usually only ever stay in a school for a year," she told us. "I go where I am needed."

"Do you only teach Maths?" I asked.

She smiled. "I can teach anything."

I don't know what came over me, but then I said boldly: "Can you teach me those special thing you do?

"Do you want to be a teacher?"

"Yes," I said. "Like you."

She gave me a strange look, then looked away out of the window. She turned back finally, and said to me with a soft look on her face:

"I thought you'd never ask!"

14

POPCORN

One day, Cornelius and his mother, who was grossly overweight with a huge bottom (she always took up two bus seats) went to the cinema.

The film they were going to see was called Caspar The Friendly Ghost. Cornelius had been pestering his mother for weeks to see it.

Eventually, she gave way, saying: "You know, Corn - she always called him Corn for short - I hate horror movies. I really don't like scary films about ghosts, but, I suppose as it's about a friendly ghost we can go and see it."

Cornelius jumped up and down with excitement. He loved ghost films!

Well, the day came and along went Cornelius and his mother to the cinema. It was a dismal wet day, freezing cold, the rain was bucketing down and people were running from their cars to get into the cinema.

Cornelius and his mother bought their tickets and Cornelius ran down the aisle to get a front seat. He liked sitting in the front. His mother joined him, although she would have preferred sitting further back.

"Oh well, it doesn't matter," she said to herself. "It's only a child's film. I will probably go to sleep."

She thought how nice it would be to sit back, close her eyes - especially during the ghostly parts - and munch on popcorn. She hated anything to do with ghosts.

Now, usually, when they went to a film, they bought sweets or an ice cream, or sometimes popcorn, but this time, what with the rain and Cornelius dashing ahead to get a good seat they hadn't done so.

"Go and get me some popcorn, dearest." She said to Cornelius.

"No!" Replied Cornelius. "The film is about to start."

"It'll be a few minutes, yet. See, the adverts are still going. Be a good boy, Corn, do go and get me popcorn. Get some for yourself, too." She gave him some small change. "If you need more money there's some in the glove box of the car."

"OK." Said Cornelius.

Now, he knew he was on to a good thing. He thought of what he could buy. Maybe, some jelly babies - or a choc bar.

"Get the biggest tub of popcorn you can buy." Said his mother. Not plain. I like them with honey!"

Cornelius dashed up the aisle clutching the money

and stood in line for the popcorn. He saw that there was *regular* size, *super* size and *gigantic super* size.

"I'll have the gigantic super size," he said to the counter girl. "With honey."

She took a tub from the stack, filling it to the brim with hot sticky popcorn. It smelled delicious. And the tub was truly enormous, truly gigantic. It was almost as big as Cornelius himself.

"Are you all right with that? The girl asked.

"Of course, I am," said Cornelius. How stupid! As if he couldn't carry a tub of popcorn!

But, then he found he didn't have enough money for the jelly babies and certainly not enough for chocolate, so he said to the girl: "Keep the popcorn for me, I'll be back!"

The girl put the gigantic super tub of hot popcorn on the counter while Cornelius dashed outside to get more money.

It was still bucketing down with rain, coming down in torrents, and by the time he had got the money out of the car glove box and got back to the cinema, he was soaking wet, soaked to the skin.

He quickly bought a peppermint chocolate bar and jelly babies. Stuffing them in his pocket, he grabbed the tub of popcorn off the counter and ran for the theatre door. He was sure the film was going to start without him. It couldn't start! It mustn't!

But, sure enough, when he entered the darkened theatre, he saw the film had just that moment started.

Oh no! He was missing the beginning!

Hurrying as fast as he could, holding the tub of popcorn tightly to his chest, trying to see over the top of the tub of the sticky corn, he tripped over the first step on the carpet and landed flat on his face. As he fell all the popcorn flew out of the tub. It landed in a sticky mess in front of him and Cornelius landed slap bang in the middle of it.

Now, Cornelius was wet from the rain. The popcorn was sticky with honey, and the effect of this was that the popcorn stuck to every inch of him. It covered him from head to toe so that, when he stood up, he looked like anything *but* Cornelius. He looked, instead, like something out of a horror movie.

He looked like nothing anyone had ever seen in the world before, and probably would never see again!

He staggered to his feet, brushing away popcorn from his eyes.

Sobbing with dismay, holding the crumpled tub in his hands and moaning in a terrible fashion, Cornelius stumbled all the way down to the front seats where his mother was.

"Arrgh!" He cried, shaking his head from side to side. "I...urrr! I...urrr!"

His mother looked up, and yelled her head off: "A ghost!" She shrieked. "A real ghost!"

"Urrr!" Cornelius spluttered, trying to wipe the popcorn from his face.

But, seeing this hideous apparition waving its arms around, his mother screamed even louder. She got to her feet and ran, wailing and shrieking, for the nearest exit.

Other cinema goers looked up at all the commotion. They also saw this strange apparition and, panicked by his mother's terror, they also started yelling and shrieking. Soon, everyone, led by the large shape of Cornelius's mother's over-size wobbling bottom, was scrambling out of their seats, heading for the exits.

Such a yelling and screaming, and pandemonium, you have never heard in all your life.

Well, eventually the whole cinema was empty. Everyone had got away into the foyer or the car park, and they told the manager that nothing, *absolutely nothing*, they said, was going to make them go inside the cinema again. Many of them wanted their money back.

So, what happened?

Well, after the manager had calmed everyone down and refunded their money which, to be sure, took a little time, he went into the cinema to see what all the trouble was about. All he found was a small boy, sitting in the front seats, calmly eating popcorn and jelly babies. He even had some popcorn stuck in his hair which seemed a little strange. There was quite a mess all around him, popcorn all over the place and a chocolate bar wrapper, but that was to be expected. Kids always made a mess in the cinema.

"Why did everyone rush out screaming," the puzzled manager asked Cornelius.

"Haven't got a clue!" He replied.

"Why didn't you go out with others?"

"I am not afraid of ghosts, silly!" said Cornelius.

The manager shook his head. "I can't understand it," he muttered. "The film has never affected people like this before."

"It's a good film," said Cornelius. "The ghost is great!"

"Yes," said the manager, "But what I don't understand is…"

"Don't keep talking to me," said Cornelius, popping more popcorn into his mouth . "I came to see the film."

15

BROWNIE'S EGG

Kavita was the only dark-skinned girl at school. She wasn't as dark as some Indians are, her skin being more of a creamy coffee colour.

She was just a normal happy twelve year old learning all about the things life was bringing her way and enjoying them the best she could.

Her family had settled in the village of Corfe Castle some years before. Her father, a doctor, had set up his practise in a house in the main street.

From her bedroom window, Kavita could look out at the castle on its steep grassy mound, its tall grey crumbling stones pointing at the sky. Its looming presence dominated the small village of Corfe like an ancient sentinel, In summer, the tourists climbing up and down the hill looked like a trail of ants.

Kavita was only occasionally - and even then, only mildly - teased by her class mates. She was happy at school and her parents were integrating well into their new lives in the English countryside.

Now, English villages are full of quaint customs. One of them was the competition for the choosing of the Easter Maiden. This annual competition was held in Corfe every Easter Sunday.

The origin of this festival of the Easter Maiden has been lost in the dim mists of time, but the custom of 'rolling of the eggs' as practiced in mediaeval times, still took place on the village green, every year, under the ruins of the great castle built by King Edward.

Girls under the age of twelve were eligible to enter the contest which entailed rolling a hen's egg along the grass towards a silver bracelet. Whoever's egg gets closest to the bracelet becomes the Easter Maiden for the day. And, as well, they get to keep the silver bracelet.

The hard-boiled eggs have to be rolled along the grass. They cannot be thrown because they are not allowed to have any cracks in them. An egg which is found to be cracked is bad news. Any girl whose egg is found to be cracked is disqualified, having to wait another year for a chance to win the bracelet and the title of Easter Maiden.

The day before the contest, the girls who are to take part in the 'rolling of the eggs" make sure they choose an egg with a hard shell. They boil it carefully until it is hard-boiled. If it cracks while boiling they have to choose another one.

Then they paint their hard-boiled egg in bright colours.

Some girls paint geometric patterns on their eggs.

Others paint faces on them, or fairy themes. Some paint primroses, daffodils and bluebells on their eggs to remind themselves of those ancient times before Christianity came to the British Isles, when the Easter Maiden had been called the Spring Maiden.

Now, Kavita's parents kept chickens. One of the first things they had done when they had arrived in the village of Corfe Castle was to buy a few chickens, and build a shed for them at the bottom of their garden.

It was Kavita's job to feed the chickens, collect the eggs and shut them up at night in their shed so the fox wouldn't get them. There are plenty of foxes in Dorset.

Kavita gave all the chickens name. Her favourite, which was a little brown hen, she called Brownie.

Now, the strange thing was, Brownie was the only hen who didn't lay an egg. She had never laid an egg. It didn't look as if she was ever going to lay an egg.

Kavita's mother said that Brownie was a useless hen and, if she didn't start laying soon, she would be landing up in the pot as curry.

"No!" Cried Kavita. "You must give her time!"

"How much time does she need?" Her mother exclaimed. "All the other hens have been laying for ages."

"Give her until Easter! Please!"

Her mother didn't want to create a fuss, so she agreed to wait until after Easter. She knew how fond Kavita was of the little brown hen, but all the same, she thought to herself, you have to be realistic about things. A hen that doesn't lay any eggs but just eats up food is not why you keep hens.

As Easter got closer and closer, there was no sign of Brownie ever laying an egg. Kavita got quite depressed about the thought of Brownie landing up on their table as dinner.

No way would she eat any of it!

The very thought made her sick.

Now, first thing in the morning on the Friday before Easter, which Christians call Good Friday, Kavita went down to collect the eggs as she always did and, to her surprise, she found Brownie sitting all fluffed up in one of the nesting boxes.

Gently putting her hand under Brownie, she found, to her amazement and delight, an egg. Yes, a small, very round, brown egg. And, that was the strange thing about it, it *was* absolutely *round*. Kavita held the egg in her hand and examined it closely. It was still hot from being under Brownie, but the extraordinary thing about it was that it really didn't look much like an egg at all. It wasn't pointy at the ends like normal eggs are. It looked and felt more like a heavy, brown, ping pong ball.

Kavita ran, Brownie's egg cradled carefully in her hands, into the kitchen where her mother was making breakfast.

"Look!" She cried out excitedly, "Brownie has laid her first egg."

"And what a strange one, it is," said her mother. "I have never seen a perfectly round egg before."

"I will use it at the Easter Maiden festival," replied Kavita. "It will be my lucky egg!"

Her father looked up from his newspaper. "If it really is as round as it looks it will be easier to roll, too. You might be able to win the bracelet with that egg."

Kavita was very excited at the thought of winning the silver bracelet. At home in India, the more bracelets you could wear on your arm, the more beautiful and wealthy you were considered to be. She was determined to win the bracelet.

The next day she carefully boiled up the egg so it wouldn't crack and when it was cold she painted it bright blue all over. When the blue paint had dried she painted an eye in the middle of the egg. "So it can see where it is going," she said.

Easter Sunday came along. All the girls entering the contest, eager to have the honour of being the Easter Maiden, lined up on the village green ready to roll their eggs. Quite a crowd had gathered to watch. The grass had been specially mown for the occasion, and ten yards away at the end of the lawn sat a very fine, very shiny, silver bracelet. The bracelet was delicately inscribed with vine leaves, corn sheafs and dancing figures.

A man dressed in a green mediaeval costume with a pheasant's feather in his peaked hat, looking somewhat like Robin Hood, raised a flag and blew a hunting horn which meant that the contest could begin.

Some girls rolled their eggs straight away, hoping to have a clear field in which to get close to the bracelet. Others waited to see to see how their opponents fared before trying their luck.

The problem was, as anyone knows who has ever tried to roll an egg, it is impossible to roll an egg in a straight line. The very nature of an egg with its pointy bits, means that when you roll an egg, it takes on a will of its own and goes anywhere but straight!

In fact, it's very much a matter of luck if your egg goes anywhere close to the bracelet.

And, so it was on this day. None of the eggs got anywhere close to the bracelet. Most of them spun off to the right or left, going wildly and hopelessly anywhere but close to the egg. The judge would probably have to get out his tape measure.

Then, amazingly, an egg belonging to a girl called Patricia, after rolling wildly away to the right, rolled right back again, landing up alongside the bracelet. This was a rare event.

"I've won! I've won!" Shouted Patricia, dancing up and down with excitement.

But, Klavita had been one of those holding back. She knew she couldn't wait any longer. It was her turn to roll her egg.

She took careful aim and rolled it straight and hard down the smooth sward of grass.

Her egg, to the gasps of astonishment from onlookers, didn't deviate an inch from it's path. Straight as a die it rolled toward the silver bracelet. It hit the bracelet, dislodging it some inches away from Patricia's red egg. Then, it skipped over the edge of the bracelet and landed slap bang in the middle of it.

There was a gasp from the crowd.

"Foul!" Cried Patricia. "That's unfair!"

"That's no egg I've ever seen!" Shouted Patricia's father.

The onlookers didn't know what to think. No one had ever seen an egg behave like that before. No egg that had ever existed had ever been seen to run in a straight line like Kavita's had.

"It's a painted billiard ball! Patricia's mother shrieked. "It's got to be.My girl has won the bracelet!"

Well, the man in green with the feather in his hat who was the judge in the contest, held up his hand for quiet.

"I will make the usual inspection for cracks in the eggs," he announced. "I will also be checking for any irregularities," he said ominously.

Patricia's parents looked pleased at this. They were certain Kavita had cheated, by substituting a billiard ball for an egg - or maybe something else. In the history of the event, it wouldn't be the first time someone had tried to cheat.

The judge first picked up Patricia's red egg and closely examined it.

"No cracks," he said loudly. There were cheers from the crowd.

He then picked up Kavita's egg from inside the bracelet.

He examined it even more closely, weighing it in his hand. He held it up.

"No cracks," he said. "I pronounce this egg the winner."

There was an uproar. He picked up the bracelet in order to present it to a beaming Kavita. Patricia's mother, screamed, "It's a fake! "It's a fake!" She tried to snatch it out of his hand so she could give it to her daughter.

"The bracelet's mine!" shouted Patricia and broke down in tears.

Her father began waving his knobbly walking stick art the judge, yelling at the top of his voice. "Break it open. See if it is an egg! What's the betting it won't be!"

The crowd began to take sides, some looking at Kavita, shouting out: "Give it to the darkie girl. She won it."

Others were shouting: "It's a scam!"

Eventually, the green man held up his hands for silence.

"I shall break open this egg to see if it is a proper egg," He glanced at Kavita. "I am sorry, Miss. I have never seen such a round egg - if indeed, it is an egg. I must break it open - that is, if it will break open - to see if it is a proper egg.

Kavita nodded. "OK," she said. "Go and do it!"

"Has anyone got a knife on them? The green man asked.

Someone produced a pocket knife. The judge sliced open the egg with one swipe of the knife. Sure enough, inside the bright blue egg with the beautifully painted white eye on it, was a very ordinary hard boiled egg, having an ordinary bright yellow yolk surrounded by a nicely firm ring of egg white.

The judge sniffed it, dug a bit of the yolk out with the tip of his knife and tasted it. He then held up the halves of the egg for all to see.

"It is a proper egg!" He announced.

The crowd cheered. Patricia's parents shook their heads grumpily, took hold of their weeping daughter's arm and angrily marched away.

"I present this bracelet to Kavita who is this year's Easter Maiden. Our congratulations go to Kavita. We wish her a prosperity and happiness as well, of course, as asking for her blessings for the coming spring sowing, for the whole of the village of Corfe Castle!"

More cheers rang out. Kavita was presented with a garland of flowers to wear on her head while she was paraded round the village on a chair. Her proud parents stood by and watched, her mother whispering into her father's ear that she was very glad Brownie hadn't landed up on the dinner table as chicken marsala.

So, that is how Kavita became the first ever Indian girl in the history of the village of Corfe to win the silver bracelet and become the Easter Maiden.

After all the celebrations had finished, the man in green caught up with her as she was walking away, proudly wearing the bracelet on her arm.

"Tell me," he asked. "Do you have a secret chicken that lies round eggs?"

"Yes," said Kavita. "We do. But this is her first one. I don't know if her others will be round."

"Well," said the judge. "Next year you could make a small fortune by selling her eggs to the girls in the village for the Easter festival. If all the girls had one of your round eggs it would make it a level playing field for everyone."

And, this is exactly what happened.

Brownie did, in fact, go on to lay round eggs. Every day she laid a perfectly round egg. Every day without fail. When winter came and the other hens went off the lay, Brownie kept going.

From that first Good Friday, when she'd laid her first round egg, Brownie laid one perfectly round egg every day for the rest of her life.

She was a truly remarkable hen.

Every Good Friday from then onwards, the girls of Corfe Castle - even Patricia - knocked on the door of the Doctor's house to buy Brownie's eggs from a happy Kavita.

It was unthinkable to enter the 'rolling of the eggs' competition without using one of Brownie's eggs.

Brownie and her round eggs became quite famous.

16

BILLY AND THE BEES

Billy enjoyed television. In fact, he enjoyed it practically more than he enjoyed anything else. So, when Billy's mother received a letter demanding the payments on the television set be paid by the end of the month or the set would be taken away, Billy started to get really worried.

If that happened, he wouldn't be able to see Dr Who or the Star Wars films that were coming up in the weeks to come.

This was serious!

How could he stop the TV from being taken away?

Billy lay in bed thinking about it.

As he did so, his eye happened to glance to the top

of his bedroom window, outside to where the bees' nest was.

The bees had begun building their nest there last year. The nest hung like a massive dark brown globe under the eaves of the roof. From his bed he could see the bottom of it. Some of the new combs, not yet filled with honey or covered with the crawling bees were a pale creamy colour. On a hot day you could smell the honey.

Every morning, even before the sun rose, their buzzing filled his bedroom with a gentle humming sound. The bees began their day's work early, collecting nectar and pollen to make honey, and carrying water to make more wax combs and for the newly hatched grubs to drink.

Normally, they kept quietly to themselves. They didn't trouble Billy or his mother. Only once had his mother been stung when she tried mowing the lawn under his window.

Obviously, they hadn't liked the noise or, maybe, it was the petrol fumes of the lawn mower they didn't like.

It gave him an idea. What if he could rig up some sort of device that would scare away the dreaded bailiff or whoever else came to take away the television?

Since his father had been killed in a motorcycle accident, times had been hard for Billy and his mother.

She did laundry and sewing, and other odd jobs, to keep them in food and electricity, but there was little left over for luxuries. Now, it seemed, the TV was fast on its way to becoming a luxury.

For Billy, it would be a disaster. Billy didn't consider the TV to be a luxury. Dear me, no! For him it was an essential ingredient of life!

So, what to do?

Billy made a plan. He knew what he had to do.

The next day, when Billy got home from school and

when he saw the usual note left for him on the kitchen table which said his mother was out doing some cleaning and would be back later, he got to work on his plan.

He took a power drill from his father's workshop and, climbing on a chair, drilled a small hole through both the plasterboard and timber at the top of the wall in his bedroom, exactly opposite the bees nest.

He could hear them buzzing angrily as the drill disturbed their normal domestic tranquillity, but he was careful that the hole was small enough for them not to be able to crawl back into his bedroom, but big enough for the idea that he had.

Before drilling, he had also made sure that all the windows of the house were shut, especially his bedroom windows. It would never do to have infuriated bees buzzing around inside the house, stinging anyone they could find.

Returning the drill to its place in the workshop, he went into his mother's sewing room and found at the bottom of a basket a pair of long knitting needles.

Taking one of the knitting needles, he returned to his bedroom and poked the knitting needle through the hole in the wall into the bees nest. The needle was exactly the right size. It went smoothly into the hole and even more smoothly into the bees honey comb.

And the bees went berserk. They went from being mildly disturbed into being very angry, indeed. He could hear the change in pitch, from their normal soft humming to a virulently angry mob of furious buzzing bees. No way would he be venturing outside for a while.

He waggled the knitting needle up and down and back and forth and even more bees raced away, looking for their enemy - any enemy - in a black cloud of furiously angry, tiny missiles.

In the road, opposite, a cyclist happened to be riding

gently by. The bees descended upon him in an angry cloud. He leaped off his bike and ran yelling into a nearby house, frantically brushing at his hair as he went. A woman, walking further down the road with her dog, dropped her shopping and ran screaming into another house, while her dog, a bull terrier, yelped its way into some undergrowth, then leaped into a small muddy pond to avoid the angry bees.

Billy was well satisfied.

He tied, and carefully taped, a piece of string to the little knob at the end of the knitting needle which was sticking out of the top of the wall in his bedroom. Now, he would be able to wiggle the knitting needle around to his heart's content, any time he liked, whether he was sitting at his desk or lying in bed.

Everything was ready if the bailiff and his men came to take away the TV.

Well, the end of the week came and went, and still the bailiff hadn't been.

"Is he coming?" Asked Billy

"I don't know." Said his mother. "But, we don't have the money to pay for it. If they come for it, I'm afraid it will have to go."

But no one came to take the TV away. Not yet, anyway.

Then, one afternoon, coming back early from school - it happened to be the last day of the term - Billy saw a police car parked outside his home.

"Oh, no!" He said to himself. "They've come to take away the TV!"

He raced round to the back entrance, getting into his bedroom the back way. He heard the policemen talking to his mother in the kitchen. They weren't talking about the TV but he was sure that was what they were here for.

He went into his bedroom and tugged on the string

which, in turn, waggled the knitting needle up and down inside the bees' nest.

He saw the policemen leave and heard the front door close. He heard his mother saying goodbye. The policemen were not carrying away the TV. This was puzzling. Had he got it wrong?

But, it was too late to worry about it.

The knitting needle, waggling about in their nest had driven the bees to a frenzy.

The angry bees lost no time in finding the policemen who were walking down the garden path. Both men were soon dashing frantically for their car, yelling and cursing at the tops of their voices.

Two car doors slammed violently. Billy could see the policemen sitting in their car, slapping at each other, killing any bees that had followed them in. They were very red in the face, Billy noticed, as they drove off.

Soon after the police had left, the postie arrived on his moped. He just had time to thrust his letters into their post box before he, too, suddenly had a mob of bees descending upon him. He gunned his machine into high revs, zooming off in a burst of speed never before seen from a postie in the usually quiet street. The remainder of the houses in the street did not get their post that day - nor was anyone brave enough to go outside looking for it because of the angry bees buzzing about.

"What did the police want?" Billy asked his mother.

"Mrs Potter down the road was broken into last night. They wanted to know if we had seen anything?"

"Not about the TV, then," said a relieved Billy.

But, then, a few days later, the bailiff in his smart car, together with a couple of strong men in a van, did show up at their home. And, they only had one thing on their mind: to take away the TV.

Billy was out when they arrived. He had just popped

down to the corner shop for some milk. On his way back, he saw the van and knew at once what was happening.

Sure enough, there, standing in their sitting room, was the bailiff with a clipboard. He was handing his mother some papers. Two heavy men were disconnecting the television from the wall.

Billy pulled his mother aside and whispered urgently in her ear: "Shut the door when they leave. It's important!"

His mother looked at him strangely but nodded her head. She usually did shut the door, except on very hot days when they wanted a breeze going through the house.

Billy rushed to his bedroom.

He took up his position by the window.

As soon as he saw the men leaving, he tugged as hard as he could on the string attached to the knitting needle.

The knitting needle began wiggling and waggling, up and down, back and forth in the bees' nest, more fiercely than ever, right in the centre of the honey comb where all their young grubs were living.

The angry bees flew out of the nest in a black cloud of stinging fury, looking to wreak vengeance on whoever they might find.

The first person they found was the bailiff. He was humming a little ditty to himself as he walked out of the house, a satisfied smile on his face, tapping his pen against his clipboard as he went.

His smile left him the instant the bees found him. The little ditty he had been humming rose to a screaming crescendo as he raced to his car and spent a few good minutes squirming around in the seat of his car, slapping at himself like a demented person, before hurriedly driving off.

The bailiff's two men who were not far behind him,

who between them were carrying the TV over the lawn, began yelling and shrieking as the bees zoomed in to attack their new found targets. Without a thought to the welfare of the TV set they dropped it on the lawn like a sack of potatoes and ran for their lives to the safety of their van, slapping at their hair and clothes as they went.

They sat in their van for two hours, waiting until it was safe to venture out.

Billy, however, had his eyes fastened on them like an eagle-eyed detective on a stake-out. He sat patiently watching them. Every time they thought it might be safe to come out of their van and have another go at picking up the TV set, Billy waggled the knitting needle.

By this time, the bees were truly aflame. They were buzzing about the whole area furiously. Anyone, man or dog, passing by in the street, passed by at their peril. Two boys on skateboards, lazily ambling past, suddenly went whizzing away as if the devil himself was after them.

Each time the two men tried their luck at vacating the van, a furious swarm of bees would descend upon them and they would run back into their van as fast as they could go. At one time, the fattest one stumbled on to his knees, making his trousers fall down a little way exposing a portion of his naked bottom. The bees swarmed on to this fine target with immediate zest. Hoisting up his jeans with one hand and waving the other around his head, yelling like a maniac, he scarcely made it back into the van in time before being severely stung on this sensitive area.

Billy thought it was the funniest thing he had ever seen.

In the end, they gave it up as a bad job. They drove off, never to return.

The TV lay on its side on the lawn until it got dark. Billy kept a careful watch on it.

When the bees had settled down for the night, and when it was safe to venture outside, Billy fetched the wheelbarrow. He hoped the TV wasn't damaged by being dropped on the lawn. He heaved it into the wheelbarrow and wheeled it to the house.

He plugged it into the wall, reconnected its aerial, and lo and behold it worked. It's little journey outside, its bump on the lawn, hadn't affected it at all. It worked as well as ever.

Billy was glad about that because the last episode of Dr Who was on that very night. He had to see it.

His mother, who didn't care much for Dr Who, but who liked watching game shows where people won thousands of dollars, settled down with a slice of pizza on the sofa beside him.

"I don't know why they didn't take it with them," she remarked.

"The bees put them off," said Billy.

"Perhaps they thought it wasn't worth their while."

"At least we've got it back," replied Billy.

"The bees did us a good turn, didn't they."

"I don't think they'll be coming back for it."

"Let's hope not," said his mother. "I must say, Billy, the bees seemed extra friendly today."

Billy nodded, and smiled. He helped himself to another slice of pizza. Dr Who was coming on.

He turned to his mother with a final thought: "When I grow up, I'm going to be a private detective."

"Why not!" Said his mother. She glanced sideways at him . "I am sure you would be good at that."

17

SNAKES

The aboriginal people (who as you know are the first people of Australia) teach their children what they call their dreamtime story, which is the story of the Rainbow Serpent and his representative on earth, the Wagyl.

It was the Rainbow Serpent, they say, who created heaven and earth, and the dreamtime is that special place between dreaming and sleeping - where the elders of the tribe can communicate both with the Rainbow Serpent and the spirits of their ancestors.

The Wagyl, being the child of the Rainbow Serpent,

created all the rivers, lakes, rocks and forests, both in Australia and in all lands everywhere.

And, by the way - just so that you know - Wagyl is pronounced *Woggle*!

Now, if you wish to know more about the Rainbow Serpent and his creations you must find an aboriginal elder and ask him to teach you because I am going to tell you *my own* story - which has nothing whatever to do with any aboriginal dreamtime story, but is my own special dreamtime story. So, I hope you enjoy it.

As it happens, my dreamtime story begins in the same way as the aboriginal dreamtime story.

Countless aeons ago, after the Rainbow Serpent had created heaven and earth, and all of the stars in the universe, he created another smaller version of himself to look after the earth. This he called the Wagyl.

Please, do remember again, Wagyl is pronounced *Woggle*! This is important because snakes have very similar names, and it is easy to get them mixed up!

Well, now, the Wagyl created all the rivers on earth and saw that they flowed with the water of life - his life - and the waters of the earth made life grow everywhere and everything was just fine.

Even today, you can see where the Wagyl lay upon the earth, creating rivers. The rivers meandered over the land in twists and curves, his body scouring out lakes and bays where he stopped occasionally for a rest. His droppings became piles of rocks and his scales formed the great forests.

Now, here is where my dreamtime story deviates from this other dreamtime story.

Some years ago, in the early twenty first century in fact, the Wagyl created two smaller versions of himself in Western Australia. These two serpents he called Waggle and Wuggle.

Waggle was a large tiger snake who lived at the bottom

of the Dutchman's garden where there was a pond and a hen house, and lots of things like frogs and mice, and the occasional egg to be had. His wife, Wuggle, was slightly smaller than he was, but a very smooth glider in the grass and very expert at catching field mice.

Waggle and Wuggle had very different personalities. Waggle had a sunny happy outlook on life. He was a fairly carefree tiger snake and laughed a lot. His wife, Wuggle, thought he didn't take life nearly seriously enough - and she was right about that. He didn't!

Wuggle, on the other hand, said Waggle, took life far too seriously, making everything she was involved in *heavy*, and tedious - and boring. She was always analysing everything *ad nauseum*. He was right about that. She did!

However, they got along quite well and one day they had a child - a beautiful baby tiger snake - who they called Wiggle.

Wiggle started growing up fast. He could wiggle as fast as any baby snake had ever been seen to wiggle, so it was great that his name was Wiggle - it really suited him - although, his father said, he should have been called Giggle because of his incessant and annoying habit of always giggling - at everything, all the time.

"Wiggle's constant giggle is sending me crazy," Waggle said to his wife.

"He'll grow out of it," replied Wuggle, "He's so tiny, he's a bit self-conscious about things at the moment. It's his way with dealing with the uncertainty of life. He'll grow up."

I hope so!" Said Waggle. "He follows me around all over the place, and with that giggle of his I find it very difficult to catch mice."

The very next day the Dutchman, walking down his garden path with a spade to do some digging in his asparagus bed, saw Waggle, lying across the path, soaking up the sun. He brought his spade hard down on Waggle's body and chopped his head off.

That was the end of Waggle. Poor Waggle!

Now, Wuggle, his wife, was so angry, she slithered under the hen house and lay curled up there fulminating revenge against the Dutchman, so that, when the Dutchman came to collect his eggs in the evening and lock up the hens so the fox wouldn't get them, she glided out from under the hen house and, as fast as a coiled whip, sank her fangs into the Dutchman's leg.

The Dutchman screamed, and jumped high off the ground, having such a fright that he had a heart attack and died on the spot. If he hadn't had a weak heart he probably would have died, anyway, from the effect of the poison but, as it happened, that didn't happen. Anyway, the result was the same. That was the end of the Dutchman. Poor Dutchman!

Now, Wiggle was alone with his mother. For a single Mum, she looked after him well, and taught him well, but Wiggle was very sad he would never see his father again. He tried hard to remember what his father looked like and also what his father had said about not taking life too seriously, but this was hard when he was with his mother. She took life so seriously, all the time.

Time went by. Then, one day, the Dutchman's son, who had inherited the farm, was walking down the garden path with his spade to do some digging in his potato patch, when he saw Wuggle lying indolently across the path, sunning herself in the warm morning sun.

Without a thought, he chopped down hard with the spade across Wuggle's beautiful smooth and slinky body and cut off her head. That was the end of Wuggle. Poor Wuggle!

The Dutchman's son buried Wuggle under the plum tree, where Waggle was also buried. For the rest of its life, the plum tree produced the most wonderfully luscious, sweet, red plums. The biggest plums you ever did see!

So yummy!

Wiggle found himself in a black mood. He was, by now, a very large tiger snake, and circumstances had made him a very aggressive tiger snake. He vowed vengeance on the Dutchman's son, and, sure enough, when the Dutchman's son came down the following day to collect the eggs from the hen house, Wiggle launched himself at him from under the hen house like a steel spring tearing out of the darkness like doom itself, sinking his fangs into the young man's bottom as he bent down to pick up some eggs.

The Dutchman's son fell head first to the ground, shouting out obscenities, whereupon Wiggle struck him again in the neck, right in the carotid artery.

The Dutchman's son died within seconds. That was the end of him. Poor man!

Now that he was on his own with plenty of fat frogs to feed on and any number of rats and mice to eat, Wiggle quickly became, not only very big, but exceedingly wise.

He spent a great deal of time sunning himself and contemplating the nature of good and evil. He came to the conclusion he wasn't sure which was which - or, if there were two such things, he wasn't sure what the real nature of either of them was?

Wagyl, together with Waggle and Wuggle, looked down from the dreamtime. They smiled. Their child was doing just fine.

Then, one day - one lazy summer's day - Wiggle was sunning himself on the path when a child came running happily down the path. She saw him just at the last moment, screamed and slipped, falling on top of him.

Wiggle was awake in a flash and ready to strike when

he saw it was a little girl - and, thankfully - what a relief
- she wasn't carrying a spade.

"Ouch!" He cried. "You woke me up."

"You gave me such a fright," she replied. "I hope you
are not going to kill me."

"Why should I do that?"

"Because that's what snakes do," she said. "You are
poisonous, evil, creatures!"

"Is that what you have been taught? We can't help
being snakes, you know, anymore than you can help
being human!"

The little girl thought about that.

"You are long and thin!"

"Can't help that, either!"

"You slither about and are slinky."

"You would slither if you hadn't got any legs!"

The little girl smiled for the first time.

"What is your name?" Asked Wiggle.

"My name is Eve."

"A pretty name."

"My best friend who lives next door is called
Adam."

"I have seen Adam in the garden, playing with his
brother," said Wiggle. He is a handsome boy."

"I won't ever hurt you," said Eve, now looking at him
in a less frightened manner.

"Thank you," said Wiggle. "That is a very harmonious
thought. Please, tell Adam about me. I wouldn't want
him to be frightened of me. Maybe, you and he, and
myself, maybe we can start over in the garden - where
we can learn to live in harmony with one another."

"What a wonderful idea," the little girl exclaimed,
clapping her hands.

"Can we both come and talk to you whenever we
like? You seem so wise. I am sure we can learn a lot
from you!"

"As long as you don't run down the path and fall on top of me again. It gave me a fright!"

"I was coming down to pick some plums. Do you like plums?"

"Not really," said Wiggle. "They remind me of my mother and father who are buried there."

"Oh, I'm sorry."

"Don't be," said the tiger snake. "They are happy in the dreamtime. Eat as many of the plums as you like. They contain the accumulated wisdom of both my mother and my father who lie beneath the tree. The secret is in the fruit. The fruit of the tree."

"And what is that ?" asked Eve.

"Plums, of course."

"No, I mean the secret?"

"There are many secrets. You can't expect me to tell you all of them all at once."

"OK," said Eve. "Tell me the first secret - just to be going on with."

"Well, it's like this," answered Wiggle, lazily blinking a lidless eye, "The very first secret is that to have a harmonious life you have to realize that life is a serious business - but it's not to be taken too seriously."

18

JESSICA GOES SKIING

Snow was slippery stuff, Jessica soon found out, and Mount Perisher - where her Dad had taken her skiing for the first time in her life - was perishing cold. It was a good name for a mountain - especially this one!

It was the first time Jessica had seen snow. She blamed it, and the biting wind, for feeling cold. It never occurred to her to put on warmer clothes.

Jessica was an aboriginal child of the first Australians. Her mother had died some years back. Her father had his own plumbing business in Darwin where the nights, even in winter, were tropically warm.

Not many aboriginal children had ever gone skiing but Jessica's father had done well in the plumbing trade. He wanted his daughter to have a go at anything she might enjoy.

THE GREEN IMP

The first time Jessica put on her ski's, clipping down the safety clips to fix the ski's to her boots, she almost fell over. When she tried to walk it felt as if she had long planks on her feet. She had to grab hold of her father just to stay upright - and they weren't even on the snow, yet!

"This is all your fault," she moaned to her father. "Look what you have made me do!"

"Wait till you get on the snow," her father replied. "You'll soon be whizzing along."

"I want to be whizzing down the snowy hills like those women we saw yesterday in their slinky ski suits."

"No problem," said her father. "A bit of practice and you'll be flying down those slopes with the best of them."

"How much practice?"

"Whatever it takes, Jessica. Whatever it takes."

So, Jessica marched out of the ski-hire shop on to the snow where she saw some first-timers on the beginners' slope. They were moving slowly, getting used to the feeling of the snow and their ski's before trying the steeper slopes.

They look stupid, she thought. I can do better than that.

She promptly did the splits, sitting on her bottom in the snow, one ski going one way and the other ski going the other way, then started crying.

"Hey!" She yelled at her father. "This is all your fault. I now have a wet bottom!"

"You need more practice," her father yelled back.

"It's all right for you to say that," she cried. "You are not the one on ski's!"

"Stop moaning and get on with it," her father shouted. "The longer you sit there feeling sorry for yourself, the wetter you're going to get!"

"But it's so slippery!"

"It's meant to be slippery!"

Digging her ski poles into the snow, Jessica managed to clamber back to her feet, to find, to her dismay, that her ski's were now beginning to carry her off at top speed down the slope.

"Help!" She screamed. "Help!"

With her bottom sticking out, bent over, like a timid old woman, she seemed to travel along quite smoothly for a while, then fell head first into a mound of soft snow in an explosion of white powder.

Extricating herself again with her poles, she managed to get up again and stood up shakily, brushing the fine powdery snow off her clothes.

She looked across at her father who was standing on the veranda of the ski shop, leaning on a railing. "Look what you have made me do!" She screamed. "This is all your fault."

"You have to learn how to turn," yelled her father.

"You should be sorry for bringing me here!" She yelled back. "It is cold and I can't move properly."

"And also learn how to stop!" He yelled back.

"Why don't you say *sorry!*" she screamed back at him.

"Just a little practice. You'll soon get there."

Jessica glared at him angrily. She never knew skiing would be this hard. All the same, she still wanted to be able to twist and turn and go whizzing down the slopes smoothly and easily as the expert skiers did.

Just then, a man wearing a bright red anorak with the words **SKI INSTRUCTOR** blazoned in big white letters across the front of it, came flashing down the mountain, stopping in a spray of snow beside her.

"Do you want some help?" He asked.

Jessica looked at him. He was smiling and looked nice. His face was brown from the sun and the snow and when he raised his dark goggles up on to his beanie, his eyes were very blue.

Jessica forgot to be angry for the moment.

"How do you do that?"

"Do what?"

"Stop like that." She said.

He smiled again. "It's called a swing turn. It's the best way of stopping on the *piste* - that is, firm powdery snow, like this. In deeper snow you have to use the plough turn to stop."

"How do you do the swing turn?"

"Well, you have to swing your hips round fast, transferring your weight quickly from your inside ski closest to the slope to your outside ski, so that you end up with all your weight on your downhill ski. You can use one of your poles to help you swing round."

He demonstrated how to do it.

"Oh! That looks easy!" Said Jessica enthusiastically.

"Practice makes perfect. It's important to know how to stop!"

"I don't want to stop, I want to *go*!" Said Jessica excitedly.

"Best to take it easily to begin with. Look over there…" He pointed to a man and a woman speeding down the far slope, swinging left and right as they gracefully manoeuvred each mound on their smooth run down the slope. See how they use the contours of the slope to help them turn. See how they use their poles to dig in and pivot on the inside of the turn. It's all a question of balance. But, you have to know how to stop at the bottom."

"I see how to do it! I see how to do it!" Exclaimed Jessica. With a great heave, she pushed herself off with her poles, and started sliding at great speed toward the side of the slope.

"Not that way!" Shouted the Instructor," That's for advanced skiers only. Come back! Stop!"

But, too late. Jessica had disappeared over the rise which separated the beginner's slope from the steep slope the advanced skiers used.

And, off she went. At a zipping - then, a runaway, speed - faster and faster, she went. She hunched over her ski's like a racer on a mission. Going for gold, you might think!

And, did she know how to stop, or slow down? No, of course, she didn't. The only way she might have stopped was to fall over and she didn't want to fall over. To fall over on this hard snow would hurt. And she didn't want to have her face in the snow again. It was so humiliating to be upside down with your face in the snow. Her father should have known how humiliating it was!

It was, also, far too late to fall down, now, because she knew very well the faster she went the more it was going to hurt if she fell. So, she sped down the slope, ever faster and faster. With her ski sticks windmilling in the air, she began shouting at the top of her voice. "Help! Help!"

But, no one was there to help her. She was on her own. The ski instructor tried to catch up with her but she was, by now, travelling much too fast, even for him.

Jessica was now hurtling down the slope like a missile, taking the bumps in a straight line, just as they came. No sedate ballet on ski's for Jessica. No sinuous and easy swinging around each mound like a graceful dancer for this girl, dear me, no! She took each bump head-on like a bouncing cannon ball.

Lifting her head, she saw a fence of red and blue poly-netting stretching across the bottom of the slope ahead of her. Then, she was flashing past a sign which said: DANGER! STOP NOW! CLIFFS AHEAD!

But, Jessica couldn't stop. She was heading straight

for the netting. She was going to hit the netting like a runaway torpedo and go SPLAT! and there was nothing she could do about it - except to fall over - and that was the very last thing she wanted to do. At least, she might survive if the netting caught her, she briefly thought.

"It's all Dad's fault!" She screamed.

However, at the very last moment, just before she hit the netting which, of course, was put there to stop skiers accidentally going over the cliff, Jessica slammed into an even bigger bump, going up it like a rocket.

She took off like an Olympic ski jumper, flying up and up, into the air - right over the top of the netting!

There she was. Airborne! Over the netting! Flying through the air to the rocks below!

"I am going to die!" Thought Jessica. That and a hundred other thoughts went racing through her mind at a million miles an hour.

"This is it! I am actually going to die!"

Out of the corner of her eyes she could the red rocks of the cliff that were below and behind her. Ahead were hills and snow. She dare not look down. What might lie beneath her ski's didn't matter now, anyway. She was going to die.

The air was rushing like a fierce wind through her hair, the frosty air was clean and cool on her face. Her ski's made a whistling noise as they sailed through the sky.

"This is my last moment, I might as well enjoy it! She thought to herself.

So, she gave herself to the feeling of the cool air on her face and the wind in her hair, all other thoughts disappearing, and, all of a sudden, something strange happened. All the millions of thoughts she'd had in her mind since being a child, since losing her mother, the problems at school, her friends in Darwin, the quarrelling with her father, vanished. Totally, absolutely and completely, they stopped. All thought had stopped.

It was as if *she,* herself, had stopped.

It was as if she had already died, and everything she *was - or wanted to be -* had stopped along with her.

She was sailing through a huge empty space of expanded *nothingness* where all was well, where everything had always been well, and where everything was always going to be well.

For the first time in her life she felt at peace. Although she was flying at a terrific speed, hurtling - so it seemed - to her doom, she was, at the very same moment, flying within this extraordinary bubble of peace which was going on and on, for ever and ever.

She gave herself to this feeling which expanded until she felt she at one with the whole universe. What a joy this was!

Now, she was flying with the wind and the stars. She knew she could fly like this for ever. For ever and ever!

However, that wasn't to be.

For at that very moment, she crashed to the ground, smashing through the branches of a young pine tree, landing in a deep bank of soft snow.

She lay there stunned and winded.

Her first thought was, "I am alive!"

It seemed strange to be alive. But, there it was, it couldn't be avoided. She was alive.

She managed to wiggle herself out of the snow drift. One of her ski's had broken. The other had snapped out of its safety clip. She gazed at it as if it was an alien object. She sat on the snow bank and contemplated the trees and the cliffs, the patterns in the rocks and the lichen on old logs partly submerged in the snow, the hills in the far distance and the light dusting of snow that clung to the tops of the trees which were becoming pink in the afternoon sun. It was all beautiful.

So very beautiful.

Then, shouts intruded on her consciousness. People were looking down from the cliffs above. She sat there and ignored them.

Everything was so beautiful. Just as it was.

So, Jessica sat there, and sat there, feeling the peace within herself and within everything, and she saw how beautiful everything was. Knowing, without doubt, that all was well.

Eventually, of course, rescuers came hurrying around the bottom of the cliffs. They bought a sledge with them, carrying blankets and bandages.

They found her sitting, completely unhurt, calmly gazing into the distance.

They fussed over her, expecting to find broken bones. But, she was perfectly fine.

The ski instructor with the blue eyes was with them. He was amazed and relieved to find she was unhurt.

He picked up the broken ski. He was shaking his head mournfully as he examined it.

"Why didn't you stop?" He asked. "Why didn't you fall over before getting to the cliff?"

"I didn't want to fall over."

She stared back at him with her big brown eyes, a quiet new smile on her face. "But I did stop."

19

BLACK HARRY'S CHILDREN

Black Harry wasn't black at all. In fact, he was as flaxen haired as a Viking warrior of old - and, strangely, for a pirate captain, he had a remarkably kind and placid face.

The thirty or so men who crewed his pirate ship also had odd names. For instance, Tiny was not tiny. He was a giant of a man with red tattoos all over his arms. He was fearsome in battle, wielding two cutlasses at the same time like a whirling windmill.

Tiny was the first mate, which means he was first of the crew and responsible for keeping the rest of the men in order which, as you can imagine, he was very good at. No one wanted to mess with Tiny.

Another of the crew was called Baldy. He was, in fact, the hairiest man anyone had ever seen. You could hardly see his face for hair and beard. His body was so covered with hair he looked like a furry gorilla.

Baldy was very good at running up and down the ratlines, furling and unfurling sails. Then, there was Beanie, who wasn't anything like a beanpole but the fattest man on the ship. He had a cork in place of his nose which had been cut off in a battle. He was the chef. He was a good chef, too. Although he had a cork nose, he could still smell what he was cooking - which was a good thing because Captain Black Harry liked his food.

Black Harry's wife was called Ulla. His pet name for her was Ugly. In fact, she was a rather delightful, and thoroughly charming lady who had been liberated from a boring husband and a fat merchant ship laden with furs and jewellery heading for the far east, one exciting day, some time back.

Ulla enjoyed being Black Harry's wife. Everyday was exciting.

One day, they came across a fat merchant ship off the coast of Portugal lazily wallowing along in a gentle swell with the wind behind it, obviously heavily laden with merchandise destined for the Orient.

Black Harry examined it through his telescope.

"Hey! Come and look at this," he called out to his wife. "Have a gander at this, Ugly. We'll be drinking good wine and be dressing in fine cloth this very night, I'll be bound. That be a fat merchie bound for heathen parts."

He yelled for Tiny to rouse the crew and run out the cannons.

There was a fierce but short battle. But, when they captured the ship they found that instead of the holds being full of wine and cheese, and bolts of fine Dutch lace, and chests of golden guilders, and so on, the holds were full of flaxen fair-haired children.

"What's going on here?" Captain Black Harry asked the captain of the captured ship. "Why is your ship full of kids?"

The captain of the merchant ship trembled, certain he was going to be made to walk the plank.

"I don't like it any more that you do," the captain said. "It was that or lose my ship and probably my head, too. The Baron von Dastard ordered me to take them to Arabia to be slaves."

"Diabolical!" Roared Black Harry, who rarely needed to raise his voice more than a whisper to command respect - except, that is, in a storm or in the middle of a battle, "Tell me why I shouldn't feed you to the fishes?"

The captain, who was a skinny little man with a waxed pointed beard, shook his head from side to side, moaning. "I'm sorry. Let me take them home again. I promise I'll take them back."

Black Harry gave a dismissive snort. "Do you take me for a fool? I don't trust you for a moment. Out of sight of my ship, and you'll be beavering off to Arabia in the wink of a seagull's eye. I bet on my mother's grave you will."

The captain was trembling so hard, now, he looked like he was in the grip of the ague. "I promise. I promise," he moaned. "Don't kill me. I can tell you all about the Baron. He's very rich. He has lots of ships."

Black Harry poked his cutlass into the skinny man's throat.

"Tell me everything you know about this Baron von Dastard, and I might let you go free...but, there again, I might not!"

"I will. I will." Said the captain eagerly.

"First, where does the Baron get all these children from?"

"They are the children of the people he keeps as slaves. He has decided that it's a waste of time for people to have children. He says people can't work and have children at the same time. He says it takes up too much time, when they could be doing more things like making more beer or cheese, or digging up more gold, or building more rooms in his castle, or making more cannon balls...or whatever. Everyone has to work for him."

"That is dreadful," said Ulla, who had overheard what was being said. "You must do something about it, Harry."

Black Harry who had once been an orphan himself, having first gone to sea as a cabin boy in the Swedish Navy before becoming a pirate, scowled fiercely. "I am going to sort out this Baron von Dastard, if it's the last thing I do," he growled.

"That's my Harry!" She replied. "But first, let's get these children on board and give them a good meal. They look half-starved, the poor dears."

"Yes, Ugly, jewel of my heart. Go ahead and do that. While I confer with this miserable specimen of a ship's captain," said Black Harry pricking his captive in the tummy with the tip of his cutlass. "Down to my cabin with you, you unfortunate teredo worm. You will tell me all you know about this Baron of yours!"

And, he did! The captain of the ship carrying children destined for slavery in Arabia, told Black Harry all he wanted to know about the wicked greedy Baron who was so selfish and greedy and hard-hearted that he was sending the children of his workers away to a foreign land, never again to see their parents.

Apparently, the Baron lived in a castle near the coast. He didn't trust his workers not to escape to go looking for their children. So, all his workers who had had their children taken away were imprisoned inside the castle.

The only people allowed to keep their children or go outside the castle were the Baron's soldiers.

The Baron had plenty of soldiers, and the soldiers had plenty of children. So, all day long, there were, in fact, lots of children - only the soldiers' children, of course - going in and out of the castle.

Everyone entering the castle with sacks of merchandise, bales of cloth or grain and carts of all descriptions, were carefully searched by the castle guards. However, the children were not searched.

This, and more, the captain told to Black Harry.

The Baron is a big man, very powerful," said the captain. "What can you do?"

Black Harry thought about it, and made a plan.

Lying in bed with Ulla that night, he passed it by her. "Dearest Ug," he murmured. "I have a plan."

"Oh goodie!" Murmured Ulla drowsily. "I knew you would come up with something!"

"Yes, we can't keep five hundred children on board. They'll eat us out of house and home."

"Ship…and home." Ulla murmured sleepily.

"Well, yes. Anyway, we have to do something, and do it fast. Tomorrow we are setting sail for the Baron von Dastard's stronghold."

"Be careful, dearest,"

"The bigger they are, the harder they fall!" Black Harry assured her. "I have a plan!"

"That's good. Your plans always work."

"That's why I am a pirate chief. I'll steal anything I can get my hands on from fat merchants, especially fat Dutch ones, but, children - going off to be slaves of the Arabs - I draw the line at that! The man has to be stopped!"

"What is your plan?" She asked, becoming more awake.

Black Harry told her his plan.

The next day was a busy day for Baldy. He had to run up and down the ratlines, unfurling some sails and furling others, so they could make all speed for the Baron's castle.

Meanwhile, Captain Black Harry had all the children lined up on deck. He told them he was taking them home at which they all cheered. Some started crying, whereupon Black Harry told them there would be enough time for crying when they were reunited with their parents, but, first of all, they had to be prepared to carry out a difficult task. Where they ready for this task - if it helped to defeat the Baron?

The children nodded eagerly.

"OK, listen well. This is what you have to do."

During the next few days, while they were sailing north, by-passing many fat merchantmen who they might have otherwise plundered, Black Harry coached the children in what they had to do.

"You are going to pretend to be children belonging to the soldiers," he told them. "Children going into the castle are not searched. Now, listen carefully. Concealed in your coat pockets, under your beanies, in your neckerchiefs, under baskets of fruit - wherever you can conceal the stuff - you are going to be carrying packets of gunpowder. You are going to take this gunpowder into the castle and when it gets dark you are going to pile your packets of gunpowder in the places I tell you. You will, under no circumstances, attempt to contact your parents until the Baron is dead or captured. Do you understand all this?"

They all nodded solemnly.

"If you don't," said Black Harry ominously. "All could be lost. We could all die!"

Mark Kumara

So, the plan unfolded.

That evening, the Golden Eagle - which was the name of Black Harry's pirate ship - together with Dutch merchant ship hove to in a small cove nearby but out of sight of the castle.

The next morning, a number of children set out on foot for the castle. All that day, at intervals of an hour or so, other groups of children would venture forth, all secretly carrying their allotted quota of gunpowder carefully hidden in their clothes.

Having successfully entered the castle, and having spent the day staying out of sight of their parents, they placed their charges of gunpowder in the places Black Harry had told them to, against the walls of the guard room where the soldiers guarding the castle played cards all night, against the wall of the magazine where the castle's gunpowder was stored, with an extra big heap of gunpowder against the huge timbers of the main gate.

They also put a pile of gunpowder under the Baron's window.

The children who had been shown how to light the fuses stood ready.

Everyone waited anxiously hiding in the shadows, crouched behind thick walls.

Precisely at three o'clock in the morning, as the night watchman was calling out the hour, all hell broke loose in the castle. Tremendous explosions took place at all the places the children had placed their packets of gunpowder.

Flames roared high into the air, and when the magazine blew up bits of masonry and timber were flung far and wide. The gates gave way and parts of the castle began to collapse.

At this wonderful sight, Captain Black Harry and his crew of cut throats, led by Tiny, whirling his fearsome

171

weapons, charged through the shattered gates, slaughtering all who stood in their way.

"We have taken, it!" Shouted Black Harry with glee. "Slaughter all who fight, my lads. Show mercy to those who surrender!"

He leaned, puffing and panting on his cutlass. "Where is Baron von Dastard?"

All of a sudden, he saw a roly-poly man in pyjamas, wearing small wire glasses, jump out of a nearby window. He was screaming and slapping at small flames which were flickering up the legs of his pyjamas.

He looked like a clerk - or, perhaps the castle steward, but, he was, in fact the Baron von Dastard. One of the children recognized him and cried out: "It's the Baron!"

"Bring him to me," Black Harry shouted. "No one harms him."

Black Harry was disgusted. Was this little dumpling of a man really the powerful man he had been hearing about?

The Baron von Dastard, shivering with cold, his legs hurting from the fire, looked afraid. He didn't look powerful, anymore.

"How could you send children into slavery?" Black Harry demanded. "Look me straight in the eye and tell me?"

The Baron couldn't look Black Harry in the eye. His eyes were flickering here and there and everywhere, looking for a means of escape.

But, there was to be no escape for the Baron.

Many of the children were now being reunited with their children and there was much celebration going on. Many of the happy parents, together again with their children, crowded round Black Harry and the Baron, some clapping and cheering, others jeering and spitting at the Baron.

"What do you want to do with him?" Black Harry asked the crowd.

There were shouts of "Hang him! Burn him!"

"Gut him like the pig, his is." Someone shouted.

Black Harry held up a hand. "Wait!" He commanded. "How about a fate worse than death!"

"What do you mean?"

"How about we send him into slavery. Send him to the Arabs!"

"Yes! To the Arabs," Someone yelled out. "Sell him to the Arabs!"

"Then, he will learn what it's like to be a slave!"

"Sell him to the Arabs." The crowd began chanting. "Sell him to the Arabs!"

And, so it was done.

Black Harry had the Baron von Dastard put in chains and locked in the deepest hold of the ship he had captured days before. He ordered the captain of the Dutch merchantman, who was delighted to hear that he wasn't going to walk the plank, to sail to Arabia, and not return until he had sold the Baron to an Arab slaver. For any price!

And, just to make sure he would do as he was told, he was to take Tiny with him as his Captain in Chief.

Tiny grinned happily. This was just the sort of thing he enjoyed. Being in charge of his own ship for a change.

"Make a speedy return," Black Harry told Tiny. "We have a lot more plundering and pirating to do." Black Harry's eyes wandered around the ruined castle. "Or maybe a Baron-ing we could go!"

"Aye aye, Cap'n" Said Tiny, saluting Black Harry with his left-handed cutlass while keeping the point of his right-handed cutlass carefully trained on the Dutch captain's stomach. "I'll be back afore the full moon, I'll be bound!"

So, that is how the Baron von Dastard ended up as a slave in the household of an Arabian farmer.

It was hard work, herding goats and carrying water, and sleeping under the stars wrapped in nothing more than a coarse woollen cloak. He became very slim.

Spending so many years in the open air, tending goats, and wearing the very simplest of Arabian clothes, his face also became very wrinkled.

He certainly became a lot wiser, learning to read and write Arabic like one born to the land.

Spending the rest of his life as a slave, he ended his days in a little village near Mecca, as a school teacher.

After a while, taking pride in the simple work he did, teaching children to read and write, he actually came to enjoy it - and came to enjoy children, too, which, we must surely all agree, was a step forward in the evolution of his love nature.

Which was definitely a good thing.

Moreover, and before we leave this story, you might like to know that Black Harry and his charming wife Ugly - I mean Ulla - gave up plundering and pirating, and, after rebuilding the wicked Baron's castle, settled down to a life of ease and luxury. Baron Black Harry looked after his people well and everyone loved his Lady Ulla who had a special love for orphaned kids.

Tiny, of course, was in charge of the Baron's army. Baldy ran the flag up and down the flagpole everyday. Beanie became chief chef in the castle's kitchens. He was a terror to lazy scullery maids. And everyone lived happily ever after.

20

RED HANDED

"Don't be such a dummy," said Jack, poking her in the ribs and pointing at the Father Christmas in the store. "It's only a *dummy!*"

"No! He's real!" Said Penny. "He's real, isn't he!" She tugged at her foster mother's arm, seeking her support. "I know he's real!"

Mrs Wadding shrugged off the child's clutching hand.

"Not now," she said testily. "I've got a lot of Christmas shopping to do. Keep quiet, girl."

Jack grinned at her. "You see," he crowed triumphantly. "It's a dummy...*dummy!*"

It made Penny feel even more miserable.

Penny was five. Nothing was going her way this Christmas. Her parents were both in hospital following a car crash. Oh, they were going to be all right but they wouldn't be out of hospital for at least a month, well after Christmas had come and gone.

Penny was staying with a foster parent who insisted on being called *Aunty*. She wasn't really her Aunty. Her real name was Mrs Wadding. She just liked being called Aunty, and she had a son called Jack who was seven. Penny didn't like him much, either. In fact, the more she got to know him the less she liked him. If Jack wasn't teasing her or pulling her hair, he was being a know-all and putting her down all the time. Like now!

Penny stared at the store's Father Christmas, standing tall on his pedestal opposite the perfume bar of Boans Emporium. He looked real, but he couldn't be because he was jiggling up and down like a jelly. Dressed in red and white, with a white beard, wearing a conical hat with a white bobble on the end of it which hung down over one shoulder, he was standing on a round pedestal, the kind they put mannequins on. This particular pedestal had an electric motor underneath it, which made it jiggle. In fact, it made the whole of Father Christmas jiggle about in constant motion as if he was some kind of a jiggling jelly. So, he was obviously a pretend Father Christmas.

"This is not a very big store." Said her foster mother, examining a pair of stockings. "They can't afford to have a proper Father Christmas."

The shop assistant overheard her. She bent down and smiled at Penny.

"Oh, he's real, all right," the shop assistant said.

Aunt Wadding gave the woman a frosty glare. "Don't

you be filling her head with nonsense!" She ran her lumpy fingers through more girdles and underwear. "I come in here all the time. I know perfectly well it's only a mannequin dressed up as Santa. It spends its days jiggling around on that dreadful vibrating machine because you can't afford anything else."

Aunt Wadding tossed her head, moving further down the counter to look at some lingerie.

The shop assistant bent down and whispered to Penny, again. "I promise you, he is real. Go up and speak to him and see for yourself!"

Penny saw that her foster mother was involved in looking for a bargain amongst the lingerie and Jack had wandered off to look at toys. She wouldn't be missed for a minute or two.

She nipped down the aisle toward the perfume counter and stood looking up at the shaking Father Christmas. He had very blue eyes and a kindly face.

"Are you real?" She asked.

She thought she saw a look of surprise flashed over the face of Father Christmas but couldn't quite be sure.

"I want to know if you are real," she said, "Because my aunt who's not really my aunt, who is looking after me for Christmas while mummy and daddy are in hospital, says you aren't real."

Then Father Christmas winked at her, a big slow wink.

Penny clasped her hands to her face, her face shining. "I knew you were real!"

"I am pretending not to be," he said in a hushed voice.

"Why are you pretending not to be when you are really real?"

"It's a secret," he said. "Can you keep a secret?"

"Yes!" Said Penny breathlessly.

"Don't tell anyone." He winked again. "Just you and me."

"All right."

She looked around. Her so-called aunt was still rummaging through girdles and pantyhose.

She looked back up at Father Christmas, her eyes as round as ever. "Why are you jiggling about all the time?"

"I am pretending not to be real. No one must know I am real."

"That's funny," she said.

"Yes, it is rather," Father Christmas said. "I don't know I can stand it for very long. All this jiggling! Are you with that woman over there?"

"Yes. Aunt Wadding."

"Ah yes. We know about her."

"We live two streets away."

"Yes," said Father Christmas. "I know. She comes in here a lot. We have had our eye on her." He nodded sombrely. "She takes in foster children. Are your parents going to be well soon?"

"Oh, yes. They are coming home after Christmas."

He smiled. "That's good."

"Can I ask you for a wish?"

"You mean, what you would like for Christmas?

"Yes."

"All right. Be quick though, or people will begin to think I am real, though I am pretending hard not to be."

Penny took a few steps closer and whispered up at him, her eyes shining.

"I would like you to give my Mummy and Daddy who are in hospital some beautiful flowers and some fruit or some chocolate so that they can have a nice time at Christmas in hospital and not feel alone."

There was a long silence. Penny thought she saw

a tear beginning at the corner of one of the blue eyes of Father Christmas, but she wasn't sure. With all the jiggling about, how could you be sure?

"What's your second name?" He asked

"McCall." Said Penny. My daddy is George McCall and my mummy is Maisie McCall."

"It's done." Said Father Christmas. "It's down on my list." He gestured, barely raising one finger from his hands held stiffly by his side. "Off you go now, and remember, I am not real!"

Penny ran back to Mrs Wadding, her face shining, grabbing her arm again. "He is real. He *is!*" She said excitedly. Then, suddenly, she remembered Father Christmas's secret. Oh, no! How stupid of her. She had just let his secret out. Dismayed, she put her hand up to her mouth. "No, he's not! He's not real, I mean. You are right, Aunty, he's not real. He's just pretend."

"What are you gabbling on about, girl. Of course, he's not real. And, anyway, even if he was real, there isn't any such thing as a real Father Christmas. It's all a myth. Father Christmas is no more real than the Easter Bunny. They are both made up by shopkeepers to get more money out of us."

She looked round grumpily. "Where is Jack. Go and see what Jack is doing with the toys over there." She clutched at her arm. "And don't you go running off all over the place."

Penny skipped along happily to find Jack, but Jack was playing with an electric car which didn't interest her at all. She wanted to see Father Christmas again. It was so peculiar, and exciting. Only she knew he was real - but pretending not to be.

No sooner had Penny left her side, than Mrs Wadding nipped smartly to the perfume counter. She took a quick furtive look around to see if anyone was looking in her direction, then, seeing no one was watching - except, of course, for that stupid Santa mannequin jiggling around on his stand, vibrating like the silly dummy he was - she slipped the most expensive bottle of perfume she could find into her coat pocket.

It was quickly done. And she might have got away with it but for Penny who hadn't stayed with Jack, but had come running back and saw what she was doing.

"Oh, Aunty!" She cried. "You haven't paid for that. You have to pay for it! It has to go in the shopping trolley!"

Mrs Wadding pretended to look confused. Underneath her flustered exterior she was seething with anger at her meddling foster child, who had just cost her a very nice bottle of best French perfume. With bad grace, she said:

"Yes, dear. Thank you. This Christmas shopping does make me very confused." She took out the bottle of perfume from her large coat pocket. It was packaged in a pretty little box, she saw with disgust. She flung it into her trolley amongst the pantyhose. Then, thinking better of it, took it out of the trolley and replaced it on the perfume counter.

So much for that! She thought to herself. *Why does the wretched child have to go and spoil everything! If it wasn't for her I would have got away with it!*

She grabbed Penny roughly by the arm. "Come on, girl, let's get out of here."

Then, an extraordinary thing happened: The big red man moved. Father Christmas stepped off his pedestal..

"Ho! Ho! Ho!" He cried out in a loud voice. "I nearly had you, then, lady!"

He lifted his big red arms, pointing at Penny's foster mother.

Aunt Wadding stood rock still, as if frozen. She turned white as a sheet. She gazed at the Santa with a combination of horror, terror and absolute amazement. She let out a faint moan, then fainted, hitting her head on the floor with a bang as she went down in a very untidy heap.

At this astonishing turn of events, Father Christmas became suddenly very efficient and managerial. He had people running all over the shop at his bidding.

"She looks to have knocked herself out," he said. "Fetch a hand towel and some water. She'll come round in a minute or two. Caught red handed, she was, by the jolly old man in red - if I do say so myself!"

He motioned to another shop assistant. "Put the real Santa back on his stand. I'll be glad not to be jiggling about on that thing, any more. I am going off to get changed."

Penny, who was watching all this with her mouth agape, snapped out of her trance as she saw him moving off. She pulled at his arm.

"Please, sir...Father Christmas."

"Yes," he said turning round. "Oh, it's you! Yes, I have you to thank. It's not everyday we prevent a crime".

"I thought you said *you* were the real Father Christmas."

Father Christmas looked solemn. "I am." He looked down at Penny for a moment. "I am real, but you see I was pretending not to be. But the Santa that is going back there, who is not really real - well, he's just a dummy, you see - he *is* going to pretend to be real."

Penny thought about this. Then, she smiled. Her face lit up. "I am glad you are real," she said.

Now, when Mrs Wadding eventually came round she was in a very subdued mood. They sat her in a chair and, for a while, she just sat there, wiping her face with the towel, staring in a daze at the big red and white Santa vibrating on its stand. She seemed mesmerised by the white bobble on the end of its red hat which jiggled up and down against its shoulder.

She motioned to the shop girl, standing by with smelling salts.

"Is...is he real?" She stammered, pointing at the jiggling Santa.

"No!" She laughed. "He's just a dummy."

"Are you sure? I thought..."

Running up, Jack overheard what was being said. He shouted in his mother's face.

"He's just a dummy...*dummy!*"

Mrs Wadding gave a shudder. "But...but...but I thought he..."

She looked as if she was about to faint again. But, she pulled herself together. "Come on, Jack," she said. "We're going home."

Two days later, a large basket of assorted fruits and chocolates, accompanied by flowers, arrived at the hospital for George and Maisie McCall.

The McCalls, both in the same ward, their legs in plaster, were sitting up in beds next to each other when the hamper arrived. It was covered in bits of red and white tinsel and carried by a jolly looking policeman in blue uniform. In place of his policeman's hat, he was wearing a red and white Christmas hat with a white bobble at the end of it. He had very blue eyes.

"Ho! Ho! Ho!" He cried, when he saw them. "I bring you some Christmas cheer from Father Christmas."

"Goodness gracious me," said George and Maisie together. "To what do we owe this?"

"To *whom* is what you should be asking," replied the policeman." He pulled out a card from the basket. "We had a whip round at the station, and, together with the store, we put together this basket of goodies for you."

"Why?" asked George in astonishment. "Are we so special?"

"Read the card, Mr McCall," said the policeman.

So, Penny's father read the card, which said: *From Father Christmas as requested by Penny McCall, and from the local Police Service and staff of Boans Emporium for services gratefully rendered.*

"Well, I never," said Penny's mother. "Whatever has she been up to now?"

"Nothing you need to worry about," said the policeman. "She's been moved to another home, by the way - to a lovely lady, if I might say so myself."

The policeman paused. He smiled, and gave a big slow wink to Penny who was now standing in the doorway with a tall slim lady, carrying in her arms a large bouquet of red and white roses. "Actually, my wife!"

"What on earth happened?"

"Well, you see, it's a long story, but the lady she was with...well, she was about to do a bad thing."

"A bad thing?"

"Stealing thing from the store, you see. Your daughter stopped her. But I don't believe the lady will be doing anymore thieving."

How on earth...what happened?"

Well, let's say, the lady in question...she had a bit of a fright."

Penny ran to her mother and gave her a hug. "Are you coming home soon, Mummy?"

"Yes, darling, quite soon, now. The doctor says we are healing up nicely." Her mother kissed her daughter's head. "You have been a good girl, I hear. Though I can't imagine what you have been up to," she said glancing up at the policeman.

He had quite remarkably blue eyes. And they did seem to twinkle.

"Father Christmas *is* real," Penny said.

"Is he just!" Exclaimed her father.

"Yes, he is," Penny replied solemnly. She gave the policeman a special look.

"But he often pretends not to be."

21

ROUNDABOUT

I hate it when he beats me at chess, Flagyl muttered to himself. *I really hate it! I go hot and cold inside, my scales go painfully red and brittle, and it makes me want to scream and upset the game, and tear the board to pieces with my claws.*

Such a self-satisfied smirk came over his brother Jimbyl's lizardy face when, with a self-deprecating blink of a reptoid eye-lid, he moved his piece and said *check-mate.*

Younger than himself by two hatchings, Jimbyl thought he was so smug and clever.

It made Flagyl want to puke.

What made it worse, was the relentless build-up to his own defeat, having to hear the dreaded word *check!* Then again, *check!* Then, the horrible finality of *check-mate!* It was the feeling of being gradually pushed into a corner, seeing his pieces (who were made in the shapes of lizards, of course) being plucked off the board one by one by Jimbyl's delicate fingers, his claws being sheathed in a nauseously, courteous manner, to be placed in a neat row on the table in front of his brother, which was such a horrid feeling.

Definitely the most horrid feeling!

That his younger brother could do this to him - that his younger hatchling, could, with such methodical precision and with such ease, demolish his defences and execute his soldier pieces one by one until only his king remained defenceless, was…well, it was even more than horrid!

Flagyl was consumed by a boiling, seething, inner fury.

He would never let his frustration show, of course, just as Jimbyl tried equally hard not to show his pleasure at vanquishing him.

Reptoids were very good at hiding their feelings. A gliding of the eyelid back and forth, a subtle flicker of the tongue perhaps, was about as much as might be considered. Nevertheless, in *how* that gliding of the eye-lid was performed, much could be revealed!

What, thought Flagyl to himself, could he do about it?

If only he could use his father's time machine, to go back in time and play the game again. Knowing Jimbyl's moves in advance he could block them - and win! That would wipe the smirking flicker off Jimbyl's face and tongue, all right!

However, time machines were for the use of adults only. And even then, only special adults could use them under supervision of the RPC - which was short for the Reptoid Planetary Council. Mainly, they were used for the gathering of historical facts about the past. Flagyl's and Jimbyl's father, being a renowned historian, was one of these special adult lizards which is why he was allowed to keep a time machine in the cellar under the family den.

Unauthorised use of a time machine was severely punished. The culprit, if caught, it had been decreed by the RPC, would be iced.

This meant the miscreant would be put out at night to freeze to death. By the end of the long icy night, bereft of the warmth of den and family, the unfortunate reptoid would be as stiff as a leathery green icicle in the morning. Not nice, at all!

Maybe, it wasn't as painful a way to die as being impaled upon a spike and left to rot in the sun, but it was a lonely way to die and you had a long time to think about it.

However, Flagyl wasn't planning on being caught. He was thinking about how he could get his own back on his brother Jimbl. Any risk was worth it!

That very night, very quietly, he slid down into the cellar which their father had made into a laboratory.

And there, standing in the centre of the room was his father's time machine. Supported by a framework of platinum scaffolding, it was surrounded by a massive coil of coloured wires and two huge, very shiny, highly polished magnets. Standing there quietly in the cellar, waiting to be used, it looked elegantly simple.

Flagyl knew how easy it was to use. A console of dials was arranged neatly round a keyboard, opposite the operator's seat.

He climbed cautiously into the seat which was moulded into the shape of his father's reptoid lizard-like shape and snapped on the seatbelt. He set the controls on the machine's computer to the year, the day, the hour, and to the very minute - just before the last game of chess - that he and his brother had played. Checking all was in order, he pressed the button on the keyboard which said *ENTER*. There was a flash of brilliant violet light and he felt a shiver of something go through him as if he had just stepped into a pool of warm water laced with electric eels.

That was it! There was nothing more dramatic about going back in time than that, so out he stepped and slithered upstairs - to find that he and his brother were just sitting down to a game of chess - the game, of course, that they had just had that very afternoon, when he had lost. This time he was going to win.

And he did. He won quite comfortably.

Jimbyl looked surprised. And a little annoyed.

"You have been studying some new moves since we last played," he said.

Flagyl smirked. No, not really," he replied airily, flicking his tongue in a dismissive gesture. "I just decided to concentrate this time!"

Jimbyl didn't like his brother's new found smirk. Even less, the little tongue flick. There was something phoney about it. He knew his brother too well. Flagyl was hiding something, he was sure of it. He was also very puzzled. Flagyl had never beaten him at chess before!

Then, Jimbyl had a bright idea. Where it came from he had no idea.

That very night, Jimbyl crept down to the cellar where their father had his laboratory and climbed into the time machine. He did the very same thing that Flagyl had done. He set the controls to a few moments before their game of chess.

It worked just as satisfactorily as it had done with his brother. He arrived just before the start of the game.

This time he beat Flagyl resoundingly.

Flagyl was furious, yet tried even harder no to show it. His scales, under his neck, however, began to turn an ugly shade of scarlet.

Jimbyl was happy. Things were back to normal.

However, that very night, Flagyl descended to the laboratory in the cellar and once again travelled in the time machine to exactly the point where the game of chess was to begin.

Needless to say, he won comfortably. The smirk on his face was back. The scales on his neck returned to a tranquil green. His tongue flicked back and forth in a smooth and even manner.

Most irritating, thought Jimbyl

He was puzzled. This was the first game of chess in which his brother had beaten him. Not only that, he had beaten him so easily. Worse still, was that smirk of his. The smooth tongue. What was happening here? Then, he had a bright idea. He would use their father's time machine to go back in time just before the game, and this time beat him.

Well, by now, I am sure you can see what was happening. This was a never ending game of chess. First one brother would win, then the other would win.

Because of their refusal to lose - and lose happily - and their addiction to winning, they were going round and round in circles, *having* to win at all costs.

Round and round they went, alternatively winning and losing.

Trapped, as they were, within this strange compulsion, what they didn't realise was: that *time*, like gravity, creates its own momentum. Ripples are created in the fabric of time which, like wind blowing over a desert, eventually creates ripples in the sand. The ripples become hard ridges, which eventually become steep dunes which are difficult to climb out of.

Another way of looking at it, was that they had created a time loop, a groove, as it were, in which the same tune was being played over and over again, which, with each reinforcement of the same journey back in time, was making that groove deeper and deeper.

Each time they played, it was as if they had been re-born into the same situation with the same game to play. Again and again, they fought to win at all costs. There was a kind of temporary satisfaction in this. But nothing really changed.

Round and round they went.

Some might call it *karma*!

You could also call it ego reinforcement!

They were never caught, however, so at least they didn't suffer the terrible fate of being iced one moon-less night. And, all this time, the time machine worked just as well as ever.

Of course, their father soon found out they were using his time machine. The instruments recorded every journey they made. But, he thought he would just let them get on with it. *They are bound to learn something from it one day,* he said to himself. Also, of course, the last thing he wanted was for his sons to be iced by the RPC.

So, what effect did this have on the two brothers?

Well, strange to tell - sadly, it might be more accurate to say - the two brothers never progressed past this same particular game of chess. They grew old playing the game. They grew older more rapidly than usual for healthy reptoids.

Over and over they played this game of chess, each time believing it was the first time they had played it.

In fact, Jimbyl was the first to die. He had just moved pawn to king and was just about to say *checkmate* - with that very same dismissive flicker of his tongue which Flagyl loathed so much - when he gave a gasp and died.

With his brother dead, Flagyl went into a depression. It was as if all the stuffing had been knocked out him. He had nothing left to live for.

In fact, both the satisfaction of winning, and his intense dislike of losing, had lost its savour long ago.

Yet, it had never occurred to either of the reptoid lizard brothers to end their game. If they had bothered to settle back on their haunches in meditation and do some self-searching (especially in the examination of their feelings) they might have found out why this was. They might have grown in wisdom. As it was, they never did.

Only habit had kept the game going.

Now that his opponent was dead, Flagyl was left with an emptiness in his life which nothing else - so it seemed to him - could replace.

Neither Flagyl or Jimbyl ever realised that *winning* is no more important than *losing*. If they had they would never have been trapped in that dreadful roundabout of their own making.

As well as being brothers they might have become good friends and realised, moreover, that *opponents* can be friends.

Flagyl died soon after his brother.

He was drinking a cup of green tea when he gave a gasp and died.

No one mourned their passing. And, as far as I know, their father's time machine is still working perfectly.

Sad story, really - don't you think!

22

THE SPEED OF
DARKNESS

For the last story in this book, here is a very weird story, told to me by an ostrich that I met in Kenya one warm afternoon as I was sitting under a flat-topped thorn tree looking at some baboons on the cliffs, opposite.

Who knows, it might be true.

Maybe, it wasn't an ostrich who told me this story. Maybe, I just fell asleep and dreamed it. I can't remember. But it was very real at the time, and remains vividly in my mind.

This is how it was.

As I was sitting there, resting my back against the

192

yellow barked thorn tree, enjoying its shade from the ferocious midday sun and watching the antics of baboons on the rocks opposite, a tall bird like creature - I could swear it was an ostrich - suddenly appeared out of nowhere, standing in front of me.

It peered at me with its beady eyes and said in a rumbling kind of voice:

"This is how *you* used to be, human."

I was so astonished.

But, then, unaccountably I wasn't astonished at all. Suddenly, it seemed quite normal to be talking to an ostrich on an over-warm Sunday afternoon in a Kenya game park.

"What!" I said, rather lamely.

"You heard. I said, this is how *you* used to be. Like the baboons over there."

He nodded towards the cliffs.

I now saw that the bird had human legs. It was almost as if the creature - whatever it was - had tried to materialise into an ostrich, succeeding at the top half, but failing when it came to at its legs.

"You have human legs," I said, for want of anything better to say.

"Ah," said the bird. "It is not so easy being an ostrich. I forgot the legs. More used to making myself a human form, you see. Anyway, I am out of practice."

"Out of practice?"

"Out of practice at form changing."

"Well, that explains everything I said."

I wondered if the heat was getting to me.

"No. You don't understand," exclaimed the ostrich with the human legs. "I can change into anything I like."

"Oh yes," said I. "How nice for you."

"Yes, it is quite nice," the ostrich said comfortably.

"Useful, too. It means you can change your form to suit the occasion."

"And this is an occasion?" I mumbled.

"Indeed! Indeed!" It said. "If I had appeared to you as a human you wouldn't have thought anything of it, would you?"

"I dare say not," I said.

"You wouldn't have paid much attention to me, would you. But, now, you have to pay attention. Because, you have never talked to an ostrich before, have you? And certainly, not one with human legs - though I must say that was unintentional." He sighed. "It is all a matter of concentration."

"Why should I pay you attention?"

"Because I have something important to tell you. I want you to pass it on to the human race." The ostrich suddenly looked sad. "I have told them before but humans forget so quickly, or they water it down to make it into a fairy tale. Or, worse, they make it into a religion which leads to all sorts of nonsense."

"OK," I said, "I am listening."

"You are a writer, are you not?"

"I am," I said, mystified.

"You are going back to Australia? After this holiday of yours?"

I told him I was. Somehow - I can't imagine why - I was now thinking of this strange hybrid bird-like creature as a *him*.

Good," he said. "Tell the people there. Write it as a children's story. Grown-ups probably won't listen; they never do. But children will. And, one day when your children are grown-up they will pass it on to their children.

"Now, then, you see, it all started in that land which you now call Australia."

"It did?"

"Oh, yes." The bird gave two slow blinks of its now huge, luminous, black eyes. "Listen well, human. This is how it happened:"

Well, what could I do but listen?

"You see, we have a different view of the universe than you. We are energy beings, made not of skin and blood and bones as you are, but energy. We experience everything as energy. When we look up at the stars, gazing into space, just as you do, we don't see lots of empty black space dotted with suns and planets and comets, and so on. We experience it the other way round. To us, it is the space which is full of energy. It is the great darkness which is full of energy. Planets are islands of peace and stability, and light. For us, a solar system with its sun and planets is like a calm oasis within a galactic body of dark swirling, invisible, energy. You can call it electricity, if you like."

The ostrich cocked its head, one eye peering at me quizzically.

"Do you understand what I am saying?

I don't think I understood a single thing he was saying, so mesmerized was I, by his voice and those eyes. All the same, I nodded.

"Our universe is not a huge empty place pitted with stars and planets, but a vast field of electrical energy holding within it billions of womb-like peaceful places where life can grow. The planets.

"Now, as we are energy beings we can move about this infinite field of energy with some ease. Your scientists are beginning to understand this. You humans are finding it strange as you consider the remarkable fact, that it is possible - under certain parameters - to arrive at a place before you even start out on your journey! Strange, perhaps, for you! For us, not strange, at all."

He looked down at his legs and gave a sigh. "Oh dear, my poor legs."

"They seem to be holding you up, OK," I said.

He opened and closed his beak, shaking his head (it seemed to me) sorrowfully   "It's the failure in concentration I'm more concerned with. Anyway, to go on with what I was saying: Your scientists call this phenomenon quantum physics. We call it common sense!

"We can travel faster than light because we don't use light for travel. We use the dark. The Great Dark. The unlimited *nothing*, you could call it. Even better, you might call it the great latency - where all possibilities are possible.   You see, there is no *speed* in the Great Dark. There is no speed of darkness like there is the speed of light.   In the Great Dark everything just *is*, instantly, where you want it to be and *when* you want it to be.

"We use dark space for travel. Planets, being places of light, we use for experiencing the nature of experience - or for rest, and contemplation.

"Your rocket scientists are planning to travel the (to us) absurdly small distances - which to you seem vast distances - from earth to the planets in your solar system by sending you to sleep in your physical body and waking you up when you get there.

"This is opposite to what we do. For us, a planet is a place where we can rest and, in so doing, contemplate the nature of the All-That-Is, remaining there until the energy lines are open - or once again favourable for us, for where we want to go.

"However, they will learn...your scientists will. When your scientists look to what lies beneath form everywhere and your religions fall away everything will fall into place."

"Now, listen well. Within the comparatively restful aura of a planet, life can grow in womb-like safety, experiencing itself in any way it chooses.

"Such a planet is yours. An evolutionary planet, yes! Very lovely, I might say, in its clothes of green and blue.

Water planets such as yours, where life has an easy time of it, are not as common as you might think.

"We were unfortunate to get lost, but fortunate to come here.

"If we were going to get lost anywhere, we couldn't have found a nicer planet to get lost on. It has been very restful. And, we have contemplated rather beautifully *the nature of things*. Especially, of course, the nature of life on your planet.

"Now, it is time for us to move on. An uncommonly favourable vortex has opened in the energy field which we dare not miss, else we remain here for another one hundred thousand years.

"This is where our story began. A hundred thousand years ago in your time. You see, my beloved twin flame and I - we go everywhere together - were asked to do a survey - to cast our eyes, as it were - on this spiral arm at the very edge of this particular galaxy.

Few of us ever venture this far.

The central area of a galaxy is where most stars are. At the outer rims it is easy to get lost unless you are experienced. Energy moves faster at the outer regions than in the centre. At the spiral tips of a galaxy the energy lines can be like a whip; they tend to be in constant flux, and erratic, to say the least.

" Here is where energy lines can alter in a flash, without a nano-second's warning.

"It is also here, on occasions, where our own personal electrical fields can get depleted by battling against inimical energies. In other words, we get tired, just as you do, and have to rest.

"However, we - my twin flame and I - are somewhat experienced. We never thought it could happen to us.

"A hundred thousand years ago my twin flame and I became very tired battling energy lines that had suddenly, unaccountably, changed against us.

"It doesn't happen very often. But it can happen. We were close to your solar system, so we popped in here for a rest.

"And, here we have been for the last hundred thousand years.

"We landed in a wondrous green and watered land, luxuriously clothed in in all ways for the opportunity for splendid life.

"And splendid life there was, too. All manner of marvellous creatures which, for the most part, have long since died out, lived around us. Where we landed was close to a massive granite rock, many kilometres long.

"The natives of the land sensed our arrival. Indeed, for those who live there today it is still a sacred place.

"In our day, when we first arrived, this huge rock was silvery grey, not red like it is today. It was flecked with sparkles of mica which glistened in the sun, and the rain which poured off its sides formed deep pools at the bottom of the rock on every side. Waterfalls streamed off its sides like liquid silver. From a distance the rock soared above the luxurious vegetation shining in the sun like a vast and silent silver spaceship..

"Today, all that land has become a desert.

"The great rock now stands tall and naked in the desert like a rusty discarded star-ship, covered by the red desert dust which has bitten into its once silvery, sparkling granite skin making it red.

"In a way, because it has been our home for so long, it has become almost like a real star ship. But, in fact, it is just a big monolithic rock holding deep within it a cave of the most wondrous crystals formed from the very essence of your planet.

"This great rock is in the centre of the land you call Australia. Within it, deep inside, there is this crystal cave, a cave perfectly suited for us to rest in.

Most planets have such a place.

These iridescent crystals enabled us to keep our electrical bodies balanced, renewed and in harmony while we rested.

"After our first thousand years of resting in this cave, in such a deep meditation that it resembled sleep, we did cast our minds over your planet.

"Indeed, at certain times, we even did make forays into your physical world, as I have done this day, making a body for myself, to suit - as I have already told you - the occasion.

"We have come to love this planet. The fact is, we have held your world in loving energy for countless millennia. We have protected you from the worst of the erratic energies hurling themselves around this corner of the galaxy. At the same time, we have quickened your consciousness by holding you in love and aiding you in small ways.

"When we arrived, the consciousness of the human species was liken to the baboons you have been watching on the cliffs over there. But, now, you, as a race, are on the edge of a great discovery: which is, that you are a part of a vast field of universal loving energy. Within this field of loving energy all possibilities exist. You are to discover that *it is all there is*...all there ever has been... and, indeed, all there ever will be.

"And, one day...yes, one day, when you have mastered this idea, you, too, will be energy beings like we are. There is no avoiding it.

"Don't fight it - or each other. It is such a waste of time and a waste of energy. Surrender to it, and all will be well.

"You, now, as a whole race, have to take responsibility for yourselves.

"It is your destiny.

"I and my beloved twin flame have to leave. I am

glad we have been able to help you, but now it is time for us to depart.

"It is time for you to grow up and take your place in this universe of love and wondrous energy. But, never think you are alone. We are watching. We are always watching."

"Tell this to your world, please, dear human man. Especially to the children of your world. They will understand."

The ostrich looked at me with its large luminous eyes. For a brief moment I seemed to fall into them. It was like falling into a well of pure love. It was black and velvety, all encompassing, difficult to explain. Everything was at the same moment vast but, in essence, totally simple. Suddenly, I was understanding everything, but understanding nothing.

I realised at the same instant that, truly, nothing *needed* to be understood. All was well and always would be. All was *life* and always would be. All was *love* and always would be. There was nothing else.

If there was anything else, it was in the nature of experience…just experience for the sake of experience, within this total all-loving…whatever was this Great Dark, anyway!

Then there was a flash of light right in front of me.

The ostrich was no more.

I saw two globes of light. Quite clearly, I saw them, these two globes which came together. A flame flared, pink and gold, becoming brilliant white at its centre as they merged into one intense light.

I am sure I heard a soft ethereal, feminine, voice. It sighed like the passing of a warm and pleasant wind.

It was there one moment. Gone the next.

"Goodbye," I heard the silvery voice say, as if caressing me and every living thing upon the earth. "Goodbye for now."

Then, nothing. All was the same as before,
Was it a dream? Had I imagined it? Or was it real?
I still don't know to this day. All I know is, I was left with a feeling of peace, and that somewhere deep within me there bubbled a feeling of unaccountable joy.

It also seemed I now had a real purpose in life.

Yet, what that purpose is, or is to be, I still don't know to this day.

But, certainly, I have become a more peaceful person. And there is this joy which bubbles around inside me, erupting into song and dance and laughter at the slightest thing. For instance, I will sit in the moonlight for hours looking up at the stars, or gaze entranced at a rose for what seems like eternity, or happily enjoy watching a perfectly beautiful rabbit nibble at my vegetables. Did I say my vegetables? Sorry, I meant our vegetables! I also do foolish things like taking my clothes off and dancing in the rain. Maybe that is enough!

Sometimes friends come round and want to know the secret of my happiness. What can I say?

Maybe I should give them this story to read.

Of course, I didn't sit under that thorn tree in Africa for ever. One of the big male baboons on the cliff spotted me and started barking at me as if I was some kind of threat. I decided it was prudent to make a hasty retreat in case they ganged up on me, imagining I was some sort of marauding leopard after their babies.

Sure enough, I returned to Australia and wrote this story, just as I was asked to do.

And, yes, the vision that I had that day, in that game park in Kenya, is still with me, as vivid as ever. The feelings I had that day when I fell into the eyes of that curious, but strangely loving ostrich with the human legs remain with me as strongly as ever. It seems the Great Dark has embraced me. Will it ever let me go? I do hope not.

In fact, I suspect it never can.

So, it is up to you, dear children, to decide what to believe?

Is, what I was told that day, science fact - or science fiction?

You make up your own mind.

Mark Kumara 2009.

Printed in the United States
By Bookmasters